Crazy Bitch:

A Portrait of Domestic Violence?

By Danielle Neves

Publisher:

Inspiring Publishers

PO. Box 159 Calwell ACT Australia 2905

Email: publishaspg@gmail.com

http://www.inspiringpublishers.com

National Library of Australia Cataloguing-in-Publication entry: (pbk)

Title: **Crazy bitch: a portrait of domestic violence?**/*Danielle Neves.*

Author: *Neves, Danielle.*

ISBN: 9780987287304 (pbk.)

Subjects: Family violence –Fiction.

Dewey Number: A823.4

For Catherine Clark, my teacher,

Christopher, my best friend

And, most especially, for all the crazy bitches

Athough loosely based on some true events, all characters appearing in this work are fictitious. Any resemblance to real persons, living or dead, is purely coincidental. Accounts of actual domestic homicides in this work are designed to alert readers to the fact that domestic violence is still a leading cause of many senseless deaths – mainly of women and children- that occur in this country and worldwide. These accounts are based on information from sources, which the author considers reliable. However, their accuracy and completeness cannot be guaranteed.

Domestic violence is a delicate dance of denial. You know what's going on and so does he. You can only keep on moving to the beat, while you pretend it's not happening.

Letter 1

In Brief: A jury has found Michael James Taylor, 26, guilty of murdering Adam Scott on July 25, 2000, in the Sydney suburb of Prospect. At the time of his murder, Scott had been going out with Rebecca Mills for four weeks. Her ex-boyfriend, Michael Taylor, broke into her home, fired a round into Adam Scott's chest, reloaded his fire-arm and walked over to Scott, who was attempting to crawl into the kitchen. Taylor fired a further round into Scott's back at close range and then told Rebecca, 'It's all over.' During the trial, police reported that Rebecca Mills had experienced 'problems' in her three year relationship with Michael Taylor.

:h inside_Updated.indd   7

3/31/2012   7:24:10 PM

Dear Pete,

This may surprise you, but every July the memories of you are palpable.

Augusts are difficult too, but- then again- my birthday falls in August (and every year I feel a little further away from the person I was meant to become!). So, here I am, as my birthday draws closer, another year in my post-Pete life, writing to you before dawn so I can hide the fact from my husband and my children, knowing I will never send this letter or even show it to anyone. Compelled to write to you; to figure out what it was about you...

There was a life before you, but I strain to remember the nineteen-year-old, rake-thin girl in that old photograph. Do you remember it, Pete? For a long time, I kept it on my mantelpiece until the frame shattered that time when you pushed me away just a little too hard. I remember you staring at me in that picture and saying,

'God, I wish I'd known ya then!' At the time, I didn't see the contempt in your eyes or the puckered lips (a man hating to accept his consolation prize). Later, the expression became all too familiar.

In the photo, I am sitting at a refectory café with four of my uni mates. Looking at the photograph, these days, I find myself searching for clues of the woman I was meant to become- before everything that happened... There are no hints in the picture.

All of us, laughing hysterically, look happy. All of us look like typical, young, cocky law students. (We are all dressed the same- button-fly Levi 501's were standard issue that year- and we are all wearing

9

expensive leather loafers that are still a staple in any self-respecting law student's wardrobe even to this day). I don't remember much about that time, except that we were all probably - as you would put it, 'tossers'- busily finding ways to throw 'conundrum' and 'precedent' into every conversation.

I'd like to blame you on heroin addiction, but I was a heroin addict, when I met Braydon's father, Richard, as well. He never used it as an excuse to abuse me. You do remember Richard, don't you, Pete? Petite, blonde, polite and softly-spoken, with delicate features (that he tried to obscure with goatee stubble), Richard was so unlike you. You were a man's man, with all the gruff joviality that goes with that. You were big-boned and bushy-bearded. You liked to wear flannelette shirts. (Don't take this the wrong way, but you were such a stereotype, Pete!)

I know you so well. I know that, if you were reading this, your nostrils would be flaring at that last comment, but here's a morsel that will give you spiteful pleasure... I have always secretly hated the photos of my wedding to Richard. Richard and I married impulsively in a hippy, new age ceremony (those weddings were still trendy in the nineties). Sometimes, for Braydon's sake, I pull out the photos of his parents' wedding. I find myself describing the event with pursed lips and a really tight smile. For my son's sake, I suppress the internal commentary. ('The purple silk caftan makes me look fat!' 'Can you believe those flowers threaded through my hair? What was I thinking?' and, of course, 'Fuck, I look so high!')

Richard and I were a left-wing nineties cliché. Richard drove an emerald green V.W. Kombi van, for Christ's sake! He managed that cool (but grungy) bar in the city. Richard had a soft spot for a derelict drunk, who bartered poems for schooners of beer and he wrote off countless bar tabs for radicals, who claimed to be communists, but were really just pot-heads, who could quote Karl Marx. (You were right, Pete. It was lucky Richard's parents were loaded!)

10

God, I loved that Kombi van! I christened it 'Oscar'. We drove that van everywhere. First, we drove it to drug dealers' places (we even left the van as collateral one night) and, later, to a methadone clinic, when we were trying to kick the habit. At the start of '97, we took the old, temperamental Kombi, spluttering, its radiator over-heating every few miles, on a camping trip to celebrate our new-found sobriety.

I am as positive as I can be about these things that Braydon was conceived in that Kombi van, when his parents were basking in the still novel, giddy, euphoria of being clean. And you will find this incomprehensibly silly, Pete, but I stood on the kerb, already heavily pregnant with Braydon, and wept without restraint (blubbered, snivelled- the works!) when the guy from the scrap metal company came to tow that Kombi van away.

Although I have spent years suppressing memories of the last year I was with Richard, you liked to torture me with stories about how low I sank, remember Pete? Sometimes, your voice feels so real and, to this day, I can still easily evoke you calling me a 'skank', reminding me of the joint bank account I plundered or the excuses I made to borrow money from friends that I've never paid back. I don't like to remember the leather jacket on the hanger in the pawn shop in the city, alongside the ring my grandmother sent me from Cuba, when I made my First Communion, but you loved throwing every desperate transaction in my face, when you wanted the upper hand in an argument, didn't you Pete?

Our town could've been a border town anywhere in Australia. The city was only a fifteen minute drive away, but its prosperity seemed light years away... the resentment for both states was imprinted on local faces like laugh lines. And that's where I found myself, when I met you... living on the border. By the time I met you, I was back on a methadone programme. Do you remember those grim, red-brick flats, Pete? We were on the cusp of the affordable housing crisis, so the rent was still just manageable on a pension...

11

Raising our son, I try to be fair, but some things I really can't help. He knows that his mother's sadness is because of his father. I never speak about our life together. When your name is mentioned in our house, a sense of oppressiveness descends, until someone has the decency to change the subject.

But every July, I remember that man, who lived two doors down from me. I loved that you said 'Saturdee' when you meant 'Saturday'. I loved that you wore one of those long, bushy biker beards and you were not in the least bit self-conscious about it.

In the beginning, I didn't even mind that you called me 'posh'. The viciousness in your tone didn't come until later. You made me feel like you were lucky to be inside me. When you made love to me, you looked me in the eye. Your breath quickened, each time you prepared to kiss me. In your raw, working-class simplicity, you must have seemed intriguing and exotic to a privileged, ex-Catholic school-girl, who had only ever played at 'slumming it'. I was, after all, not even twenty-five years old.

There's a photograph you took of me that July, when we first came together, remember? I'm wearing my hair in pig-tails and I look so heart-breakingly optimistic. The furniture I have filled my flat with looks thread-bare and second-hand. My surroundings are bleak, but my face is filled with the hope you can only muster when you are in your twenties. I love that photo of myself, Pete. In July, the longing is an ache... to be that girl again- nearly twenty-five and full of faith.

V

*

Not much to do 'ere. I find meself thinkin': a lot; much more than I 'ave in years. I'm doin' a lotta readun and gettun pretty buff as you do, in here.

In July 2000, she was gettun out of the detox ward. She was tryin' to save 'nuff money to move into those flats I lived in, aimin' to have enough money saved by mid-July. If she'd just chosen somewhere else to live or had been knocked back by the real estate agent... I wouldn't be here. As weak as it sounds, 'er decision changed me life.

Steve, sometimes, I reckon this is a dream. This is somethin' that should be happenin' to someone else. Not to me.

It's funny, but when I see the tattoos on me arms that brings me back. I know it's fucking real. I got these stupid tatts when I was still with her. I feel the blue lines on me arms and I know this is fucking real.

Sorry, mate, I know you've heard this story before, but, Steve, I'm in jail for life. Not just life; that fucking judge sentenced me to additional time, 'never to be released'. I just don't understand how this can be happenin' and I need to tell someone... make some sense of it. The one person I wanna talk to about all this stuff... well, I can't talk to 'er anymore. I'm sorry, mate, you're me brother; you may not owe me anythun, but I need to get my side o' the story out and I guess you're it.

I've read the transcripts over 'n' over. When the judge sentenced me, 'e said,

'Never in my career have I confronted such an appalling case of premeditated violence. This murder serves as a sobering reminder that our society is still grappling with the scourge of domestic violence.' Well, Steve, it wasn't always like that, man. There were good times …

*

James Blunt's a fag, but ev'ry time I hear that line, in that song, *You're Beautiful*, it reminds me of 'er. Ya know, how he sings about the girl catchin' 'is eye as he walked by. Well, the first time I saw 'er, it was just like that. Comin' home late from the pub, walkun past her joint to me flat, her blinds would never quite shut all the way and I could see her asleep in the livin' room. She had skin the colour of a weak cuppa coffee. Ya could tell just by lookun at 'er, her skin would be deadly smooth. She had that dark, long, wild hair all over the pillow. God, I wanted a piece of that.

She ruined me life and, Steve, I know you still dunno what I saw in 'er. But she was the one, mate. She was the mother of me kid. She was the love of me life and it started in that moment, when I perved through the blinds, slightly pissed, at this gorgeous chick two doors down sleepun on a sofa bed in her livin' room. I'm no fuckin' Shakespeare and maybe I'm not explainin' it right, but I kinda knew in that moment that she was the one, the only woman I was ever gonna love.

And this'll sound fuckin' crazy after everythun that's happened, but I love her still. When I soap the blue Celtic 'V' tatt on me arm, I think of her. When I look in me son's eyes in the photo stuck up on the wall of me cell, I want her so badly, mate.

*

The first time I heard 'er voice was two days after she'd moved in. Two doors down.

Her voice had a hint of posh in it. She hadn't grown up local. She had gone to a good school, you could tell.

14

She was carryun some washun in from downstairs 'n' I was in 'er way as she tried to walk past me on the walk-way. It was narrow so she said,

'Excuse me,' I introduced meself.

'I'm Pete,' I said. She put down the washun basket, I remember, held out 'er hand 'n' told me 'er name,

'Nice to meet you,' she said shakin' me hand 'n' smilin' this bloody, big brilliant smile. I remember thinkin', 'What the hell is this chick doin' here?' I remember just knowing she was outta her depth, mate.

Remember how they used to call it 'struggle town' 'coz no one could get a job and everythin' was such a fuckin' struggle? Well, you couldn't forget it was a struggle in those flats! Carpet that smelt mouldy and was all worn 'n' seedy 'n' grey and the kitchen wasn't much bigger than this fuckin' cell. It was tuff to fit a proper-sized bed in the bed-rooms. She was a city chick from a rich family so she didn't get that a good-lookin' chick livin' by herself in a crappy flat surrounded by *those* fellas couldn't be that friendly. Talkun like she was talkun to me in front of those guys was just askin' for trouble, if ya know what I mean.

I guess I couldn't resist the fact that she was so trustun. Thinkin' back now, I dunno if it was an act or not. All I know is it made her so hot to me.

It's funny, mate. I was with 'er for two years, but she was fulla surprises, ya know. Like, sometimes, she could talk tuff and swear like a bloody sailor. Then, when she wanted to, she would talk smart with her big words and lord it over you. About some things, she was a fuckin' clueless slut and about others- like taxes 'n' the law 'n' shit- she was bloody brilliant! Ya never knew what to expect, if ya know what I mean.

She was on the methadone then and ev'ry mornin' she trekked up the street to go to the clinic, but she didn't have that hardness about her like some of those 'done chicks that lived in our flats. Her skin was still smooth and 'er smile was still sweet; not hard. Maybe, she done some things she regretted, while she was on the gear, but I could tell she'd never been a hooker. She woulda been wiser about stuff if she had been.

In the days before I got with 'er, I was a decent, ordin'ry bloke. I liked a punt. I lived for the football season. I enjoyed a bong and I liked me beer. I don't care what the newspapers said, that's not nuff to make me a psychopath.

Me mates called me Lloydee, Mum 'n' you 'n' the rest of the family called me Pete. I did all right in school, dropped out before finishin' me high school certificate and I loved me rugby. Then I did me apprenticeship. 'Couldn't find work locally so I moved to Sydney and was a labourer for a bit there. I had me own place, a nice car, a good stereo and I didn't mind a stab at the pokies on pay-day. I reckon I'd still be there - livin' the good life - if that fucking junkie scumbag hadn't held me up with a syringe.

After that, everythin' went to shit. Lost me job, hadda move back to live at Mum's and started smoking pot… couldn't get another labourin' job, so I went on disability. By the time I met 'er I was livin' in this fucking tiny flat, 'coz Mum had kicked me out. They were the crappiest flats! Fulla losers on the dole or on disability; guys just outta jail, speed freaks, a coupla heroin addicts… the place was a dive!

She told me the story, later, when I got with 'er. The first week she moved in, a cop car pulled over, while she was walkun 'ome from the shops.

'We've seen you around here a bit. Got an explanation for that?' They musta thought she was a dealer, or somethun.

'I live here,' she said. That stopped 'em cold for a second.

'Pretty rough place to be living…'

'I've been homeless. It beats the hell out of that,' she said. I can imagine her sayin' it too, with a smile and in a smart ass voice. She'd been a law student. She wasn't gunna be intimidated by the cops. Like I said, mate, sometimes she could talk tuff.

She laughed, when she told me that story, but she didn't get it. Ya could tell she didn't belong there- just lookin' at 'er, ya know. It was in everythin' about 'er. Her clothes looked pricey. She didn't talk like the rest of us 'n' she held 'erself differently, if ya know what I mean.

I guess I've always had a thing for chicks like that- girls who're outta me league 'n' a little bit cool. (Remember how I got that major crush on Jodie Foster after *Silence of the Lambs*?) Lotsa times, I used to get up the courage to talk to chicks like that by drinkun, but then I was too pissed to make an impression. With her, it was different. She was posh, but she didn't seem like the kinda chick that would look down 'er nose at ya.

And there was somethin' so fragile 'bout 'er- like 'er heart was broken or somethin'. But when she smiled – fuckin' hell! It was awesome mate! And I know it's hard to believe, but when I first got with 'er, she smiled heaps.

It was fuckin' crazy. She was livin' in that shit-hole, stayun off smack, flat broke, but the chick could still smile. She'd get all excited 'bout some line she read in a book or she'd find some bargain at an op shop and 'er eyes lit up.

But there was always that damaged side of her too. That's why she was livin' there, after all. When I think 'bout it, I guess it was that fucked-up bit of her that brought us together.

17

I mean, the first night she came over she was off 'er face, her pupils were like pin-pricks.

'Can I hang out here for a while?' she asked; 'er voice all slurry 'n' slow. She had that slow, sleepy, noddin' off voice 'n' look that junkies get when they just hadda shot. 'I just don't want to be alone right now… I've had a shit of a day.'

'Yeah sure, wanna talk 'bout it?'

'Not particularly,' she said, barely able to keep 'er eyes open. She was *so* out of it.

She nodded off on me sofa. We've all been there, Steve. Ev'ry man's done it. A chick's a bit *too* wasted to know what's goin' on, ya know. I couldn't help meself. I unbuttoned 'er top. Her bra was real bright, I remember; this deep, deep red thing with a clasp between 'er tits. I unlatched it, mate. She was so fucking high, so fucking sad and her tits were so fucking beautiful.

I sucked her big brown nipples, while she was passed out on me sofa and got so hard I coulda come there and then. She came to, while I was debatin' with meself whether to go all the way. She looked at 'er bare tits for a sec, tryin' to remember, but she was so wasted she couldn't. She 'ad no idea what she'd done or hadn't done. She looked at my hard-on and then looked into me eyes, searchun for somethin'. Her face was so sad, mate.

'I miss my son,' she said and the look in her eyes was so far away, 'and I miss the life I had.' She focused on me then with those tiny pupils. For just a sec, she looked totally straight. I kissed 'er then- hard. She didn't pull away. I rubbed my hands over 'er tits 'n' she let me.

Then, just like that, she puts on 'er clothes, kisses me on the mouth and goes home! Freaky bitch! I thought 'bout 'er tits that night,

18

wanking extra hard, wantun to be inside her. Ya know I can see that neat, clipped triangle in me head now and ev'ry night I'm in 'ere and it is agony, man!

She slipped a note under me door the next day. Neat hand-writin', blue biro, purple paper, it read:-

Sorry. I was so wasted. It won't happen again.

Me heart fell. I'm not like you, Steve. I'm not good with women and I'm not smooth. I drink to get up the courage to talk to 'em 'n' then I get so pissed only the most ugly, desperate whores will talk to me. I'm pissed enough, by then, that it's all right.

This chick was different. Ya get a shot at a chick like that once in ya life. Ya gotta take it, mate.

One day, she came by to borrow somethin'. I can't remember if it was milk or sugar. I'd just finished mullin' up some pot and I offered her a smoke.

'No thanks, I don't smoke,' she said. Then she looked all uncomfortable 'n' sorry 'n' sad. 'Sorry. I didn't mean for it to sound like that. I'm being really, rude. Shit! Sorry! Look, I honestly don't mind if you want to. Marijuana's just not my thing.' That was 'nother surprise. I woulda picked 'er for the kinda chick that woulda smoked, snorted, swallowed and shot up anythin' that come 'er way, but I was wrong. I found out later she had no problems with bangin' up smack, coke or speed, but she was a precious snob when it came to weed 'n' pills 'n' alcohol.

I didn't feel right smokin' by meself, so when I said what I needed to say to 'er, I was almost totally straight. It was 'arder than I thought it was gunna be. I was pretty nervous-like, me voice was breakun up a bit, but I took a deep breath 'n' went for it.

'You know, I *want* it to happen again.'

And that's how it started, mate… In me gut, I knew it was a mistake. She was damaged goods, but she was still outta me league. She was gunna wake up one day 'n' know she was better than this. She was gunna break me heart, one day. Like I said, deep down, in me gut, I could tell, it was a mistake.

But it's like that sometimes, isn't it Steve? Ya get a chance like that once in a life-time. I hadda take a shot. I shoulda known better, but I couldn't stop meself.

20

Letter 2

In Brief: Sargon Younan was convicted of murder yesterday in the Victorian Supreme Court. On August 22, 2000, Younan bludgeoned Victoria Skidmore to death with a garden fork in a car-park in the Victorian suburb of Doncaster. Ms Skidmore had broken off her relationship with Mr. Younan three weeks earlier because of his 'extreme jealousy.' Before killing her, Mr. Younan sent Ms Skidmore a text message reading: 'If I can't have you, no one will.'

ch inside_Updated.indd 21   3/31/2012 7:24:13 PM

Dear Pete,

*L*et me tell you about recovery the second time round. Recovery without Richard...

One weekend, I wallowed in uber nostalgia. Missing my green, Kombi van life desperately, the cravings stronger than longing for a limb, I read Trainspotting *by Irvine Welsh,* Junkie *by William Burroughs and Anne Marlowe's* How to Stop Time: Heroin, an A-Z (*in one sitting!*).

I gave myself permission to remember, wrapping myself in the warm, rose-coloured recollections evoked by the phrases of wordsmiths, who wrote with a grim authenticity I know, from experience, can't be faked. Clinging to authors, who understood me, I indulged in reminiscence.

I still give in at times. Don't misunderstand me, Pete, I haven't touched a needle since I left you, but I still keep a really old, worn, dog-eared copy of Michael Dransfield's Drug Poems *on my book-shelf. Sometimes, at odd moments, I reach for it. Curled up on my sofa, I can be absorbed by the poetry for hours.*

Once, when he was about six, our son, Michael asked me,

'Will you read to me from your favourite book Mummy?' I was staunch when I refused, slapping the paper-back covers shut, returning it guiltily to the book-shelf; up high, where there was no hope he could reach it.

Most days, I can find solace in the ordinary- children's soccer games, a glass and a half of really shit-hot good, red wine, a particularly tender steak, a moderate love affair based on shared histories and common electricity bills, car payments and debriefing about office politics.

Normally (though not in July), I can forget that warm rush to the head that erases all other sensations. I can forego passion that leaves your whole body throbbing and marked in the purples and greys of masculine rage. A life devoid of extremes gets easier with time.

The year I met you… well, relief was harder. Morning routines engulfed an hour or two of yet another interminable day, when I wasn't going to be scoring smack. I tried to find comfort in the pedestrian- putting on a beautiful, long, A-line, purple silk and lace, beaded skirt, which flirted with my ankles and matching it with Doc Martens, I reached for that giddy frivolity of first-time sobriety I had once found with Richard and found myself wanting.

Every day, I skulled a hasty, luke-warm instant coffee without milk or sugar and then I began the long, three-block trek up-hill to the methadone clinic. Every day, no matter what the weather was like, I sweated all the way there- hence, those singlets you told me made me look slutty.

I had my daily dose. I was on a rapid reduction regime so my dose was a little slighter every day. I waited the half hour until the cramps in my stomach stopped and the soreness in my shoulders and lower back eased, then I walked to the bus stop.

It was only an hour-long ride and two bus trips, but it felt endless. Every block of flats I passed seemed to remind me of scoring or scamming so I could score or had some hidden corner in the garden, where I had furtively shot up a wack I was desperate for. I learnt to submit passively to the gritty slide-show of memories. It was worse when I tried to shut them out; as if my resistance to these images increased their potency.

I used to get off in the city to catch my connecting bus. My bus-stop was in front of a pricey furniture shop. The shop is still there if you can believe it, Pete! Most of the trendy cafes have gone out of business, but the Thai restaurant is still there. It has survived long enough to be legendary.

Waiting for my connecting bus, I stood across the road facing the large windows of the two-storey, dark, brown-brick, courtyard flat at the government, housing commission complex that had, at one time, defined all my horizons and aspirations. Flannelette sheets served as curtains.

They've torn down that complex now. (I am so grateful for that fact every time I drive into the city to visit my mother- otherwise, the memories would be too brutal for my visits to be as frequent as they are!). The image of that flat that once haunted me is difficult to picture clearly now, but I can still readily recall the feeling of facing that flat, while I waited at the bus-stop (like the sensations are hard-wired into me). Standing at the bus-stop, feeling the grubby weight of memories of divine hits of beige heroin, it took every ounce of restraint to focus on the task at hand. Every time, I made the second leg of my trip, the crooks of my arms twinged all the way.

At every bus stop, I silently dared myself to throw restraint to the wind and embrace escape. I gave myself permission to ring the bell and stop the bus and get off it and keep on walking towards oblivion.

I was always a little surprised at myself for getting off at the right stop, without jumping off early. I walked into the child-care centre, surviving the judgemental stares, the pitying tsks, tsks, the nostrils flaring with barely disguised disgust... His face always lit up.

'Mummy!' For a tortuously brief hour, there was nothing else but him. He always screamed hysterically when it was time for me to go.

I always performed the last ritual by rote. I would wave goodbye to him, and, then, without thinking about it, I would turn away and keep on walking. It would have broken my heart otherwise.

One night, you averted your eyes, cleared your throat and clumsily told me - with the goofiest of smiles - that you wanted to kiss me again (the memory of that smile still makes me grin). Relief was hard to come by. I'd like to blame you on heroin, but that would be too easy, wouldn't it? Granted, I was in recovery, and I took my endorphin rushes any way I could get them, but I can't blame you on heroin. You'd call that a cop out, wouldn't you, Pete? As much as I hate to admit it, I fell in love with you.

26

V

*

I've been tryin' to work out what it was about 'er. I know you hated 'er the first time ya met 'er. You told me the first time ya saw 'er, 'That chick's bad news.' Maybe, you were right, mate. Yeah, she came with a lotta baggage, that's for sure.

Did I ever tell you the story of how she ended up there? Two doors down?

Well, she was raised richie-rich. She went to a good school, 'n' she was smart. She got into law. But, in her last year of uni, she got hooked on smack 'n' dropped out.

She met her son's dad 'n' married 'im. She showed me the wedding shots. She was wearun a purple dress and she looked high as a kite. He was a junkie too, but he 'ad a good job, earnt good money 'n' came from a rich family- like 'ers.

I know you reckon once a junkie always a junkie, but, ya gotta understand she'd been a junkie, but she wasn't ya typical junkie low-life. Mate, she 'n' 'er ex had been loaded compared to most other junkies. So, they may o' been junkies, but they were never gunna be shootin' up smack 'n' livin' on the street, stealin' 'n' beggin' for bus money, like most junkies ya see 'round the place. They both 'ad jobs 'n' rich families, ya know. They were always gunna 'ave nuff money so they didn't sink as low as other junkies have to.

She told me that they got into a methadone programme when they'd 'ad enough. She told me they had a son, Braydon. She got real sad before she told me the next bit, Steve.

She went back to smack when Braydon was one. This time it was different for 'er.

She worked three jobs 'n' pawned all 'er son's baby stuff. She was cryin', when she told me. Her tears were hot, mate and she was fulla shame, when she told me.

'I can still remember standing in the pawn shop. It was a vintage toy, you know. I knew it was worth a fortune. Braydon's grandmother had brought it back from her trip overseas, Pete. They offered me twenty dollars.' She cleared 'er throat, 'I needed a hit. I took it.'

Braydon's dad dumped her, when 'e found out she was back on the gear. She was homeless for a bit, before she landed in the detox ward. Now, she was back on the methadone and tryin' to start over.

She smiled when she told me that last bit. I'll never forget it. Eyes red from cryin', naked in bed ('coz we'd just fucked), she'd just told me a story that could make any guy with half a brain walk out the door. I felt real uncomfortable 'n' I kind a mumbled 'n' I asked 'er,

'Why d'ya keep all these photos of that time layin' around?' The chick smiles 'n' says,

'There are some things that hurt to remember, Pete. Those are the things I can't let myself forget.'

So, there I was, Steve with this hot chick, who was – by 'er own fuckin' admission- damaged goods. Why didn't I just get laid 'till I got sick of 'er 'n' fuck off? What was it about her that kept me goin' back for more o' her abuse? Was I just thinkin' with my dick? You asked me that one time, hey? Was that it? I gotta say the sex was amazun, but I don't think that was it.

I been tryin' to figure it out. Like I said, I gotta lotta time to think in 'ere.

I reckon it was this. She made me feel like shit with a look, sometimes. She could make me want her like crazy even when she was just yawnun. Sometimes, she made me angrier than anyone's ever made me in me life. Other times, her smile... well, I told ya about that, before.

Sometimes, I wonder what the hell I was thinkun. I mean mate, I knew the story of all 'er scars at the end of the first week I fucked 'er. If she was that open with a story fulla shit that you'd have good reason to be shamed about, how easy was she with other stuff? A woman, who was that open hadda be suspect, right, Steve?

She used to wear those skimpy strappy singlets, remember? She used to put elastics in her hair and wear l'il pigtails. She wore those long, see-through, hippy skirts, remember? She looked like a slut. I told her so, a l'il while after I started sleepun with 'er.

I did it nicely of course. I'm not stupid. I said,

'Why d'ya wear the clothes ya wear?' She knew what I meant. I mean she dressed pricey, but she still always looked so fuckin' sexy. It made me wonder who she was out to impress, ya know. She looked at me sharply, 'er chin juttun out.

'What do you mean?' she asked.

'You know what I mean. You know ya don't wear *normal* clothes.' She did that 'victim' thing, you know. Shrugged her shoulders, licked 'er lips 'n' sagged a bit.

'I didn't know you hated what I wear so much.'

She started dressun less slutty. I didn't think she was gunna change, but she did. This girl from the city from a good school 'n' a rich family, changed what she wore because she didn't want me to call 'er a slut. Havin' that power over 'er made me want 'er even more. Plus, it meant she gave a damn. In the end, it got to the point I needed her to prove that a lot.

So, maybe in the begginin' it was the sex. But after, I guess I just knew I was never gonna be with someone like her again. It scared me 'n' I didn't wanna lose her. Sometimes that drove me a bit crazy, I guess.

I 'member the first time I made 'er cry, mate. Like I said, she could make me madder than anyone I ever known.

Remember, the way she walked- invitin' you to fuck her 'n' those 'come fuck me' eyes? You better believe I called 'er on it! 'Bout a week 'n' a half after I started sleepun with 'er, I said to her, while we were lyin' in bed, kinda snugglin',

'You want 'im don't ya?' She looked at me, all innocent, like,

'Want who?'

'You want Steve.' She smiled and that gave it away, mate.

'You're kidding!' she scoffed. I didn't buy it for a second, matey.

'Aw come on, it's in the way you walk and talk when you're 'round 'im… I'm not stupid!' She did that 'victim' thing again. She looked all uncomfortable and sad. To this day, I dunno if that look was an act with her.

'I'm with you,' she said.

'Are you? Are ya *really*?' Maybe we're *just fucking*? Maybe this is just a game for you. Slummin' it, are ya, rich girl?' She started crying, 'er whole body shakun,

'How can you think that about me, Pete? I like you. I like you a lot. I'm not sleeping with anyone else and I don't want to. I wouldn't do that to us.'

Just like that, I felt like a prick. When she cried, mate… I always felt like shit. I hated it when she got me feelun like that. I held her,

'I'm sorry babe. I just want you so much it drives me crazy sometimes, hon 'n' you're so fuckin' hot. Who wouldn't be jealous?' She laughed then and that shit feelun was gone.

There's somethin' addictive 'bout bein' with a chick like that. She makes ya feel like shit one minute and king of the world in the next. Sometimes, I felt like I was gettin' as crazy as she was, but other times I watched 'er when she was sleepun or doin' somethin' 'n' she didn't know I was watchun, I just got hard as. Love like that… it's a bitch. I guess that's why I'm in 'ere, mate.

Letter 3

In Brief: David Vance Mizon, 42, has pled not guilty to murdering Lucille Rosalie May, 40, at her home in suburban Melbourne on September 10, 2000. Mizon allegedly stabbed his pregnant girlfriend sixteen times, before leaving the scene. It is alleged that Mizon then returned to the scene and contacted police, claiming to have 'discovered the body'. Police report that their suspicions were raised by the cuts on Mizon's hands.

ch inside_Updated.indd   33

3/31/2012   7:24:15 PM

Dear Pete,

Becase I have been prolific (that is a much nicer word than 'obsessive') about documenting my family's history, I have many baby photographs of both my sons. And, since I left you, I have been moderate (but thorough) about photographing the school assemblies, birthdays and other significant mile-stones that 'good' mothers should capture with their digital cameras.

There are also many photographs of Braydon's father, flirting with the identity of 'Dad'. In my favourite one, a younger Richard with dread-locked hair (he has had the good sense to relinquish the dreads now that he is older) is barbecuing tandoori chicken wings, whilst holding his infant son. It is true that my photographs of Richard are not on display, but they can be fished out from old albums (they exist, in other words!).

Of course, (although this will make your upper lip curl) there are many photos of my husband and me. I have devotedly documented my post-Pete life with snap-shots of birthdays, weddings and holidays.

But, I haven't kept a single photograph of you, Pete. And, now, our son, Michael, is getting old enough to notice the incongruence.

If the truth be told, I can only remember ever being photographed with you once, Pete. I think your mother took the snap-shot and I remember it clearly, even now, years later.

In the picture, I was dressed in dark purple, satin pyjamas and you were sporting one of your trade-mark flannelette shirts. You and I were sitting on a hospital bed. The photograph was taken just after

35

Michael was born. You were holding Michael and looking into his eyes. Pete, the expression on your face -there's no other way to describe it- you looked captivated.

And I remember this about that photo vividly, Pete (even though I don't have a copy to refresh my recollection)... while you stared into our new-born son's face, I was looking at you. I looked weary, but serenely happy and I felt moved to touch your face, when our son, Michael was born.

Struggling to understand what was so irresistible about you, I have compared notes with other survivors. One woman I know speaks of 'a honey-moon phase' and lavish gifts of flowers, designer jewellery and chocolates. She showed me a bracelet and I did not have the heart to tell her that it was an obvious knock-off.

I have searched diligently for memories. There were certainly fragments of charm, but there was never any 'honey-moon phase' with flowers, jewellery or chocolates (we were dirt poor, so your romantic appeals came unadorned, didn't they, Pete?)

Nonetheless, I do have one favourite memory of our early time together. I had rushed into your flat, girlishly excited one afternoon, carrying a plastic bag containing a bargain I had found at an op-shop. When I had spotted it, I had been unable to resist the black, velvet, fully-lined, full-length halter-neck dress. It had the kind of A-line skirt that Marilyn Monroe had made famous standing over a vent... and, it had only cost me six dollars, Pete!

When I modelled that dress for you, you said,

'Ya look great!'

But you saw something else too, didn't you? That I would never have occasion to wear it...

So, when you had a big win on the club poker machines that spring, you were attentive enough that you thought to take me out to an expensive restaurant, where I could show off my sexy, new dress. It may surprise you that I have kept the dress all these years (it probably wouldn't fit me anymore, but that's not the point, is it Pete?) Perhaps, one day I will find the gritty reserves to share stories of these glimmers of your sweetness with our son. But, Pete, try to understand… I can't do it now. Not just yet.

V

*

Mate, everybody goes on 'bout how it ended 'n' everyone wants to figure out when it started to go wrong. Sometimes, in 'ere to pass the time, I like to remember the good bits, ya know.

She was a class act, ya gotta give 'er that. She bought this black dress once 'n' I took 'er out to dinner. Fuckin' hell, mate! Every guy in that joint was lookin' at 'er, but she just kept lookin' at me and talkin' to me, while we were eatun. Like she couldn't tell that she looked hot as. I loved that about 'er.

And plus, there was this. When I needed 'er, she was there for me.

I never told ya this, Steve, but I got picked up for possession pretty early on in the piece after I started seein' her. The coppers gave me a choice- rat or get locked up. Fuckin' pigs! It was a measly twenty bucks worth of shit, if ya can believe it?!

I hadda rat on me mate, Gazza. Fuck, I felt like a prick!

And there was not a soul I could tell, 'xcept her.

'You did what you had to do, under the circumstances. You can't think that Gazza would not have done the same thing, if he were put in the same position...'

'He's gunna know, babe.'

'Not from me, Pete and not from the police. The best thing you can do is let it go.'

Tellin' 'er helped me face Gazza without flinchin'. I never did 'fess up to what I done and I don't think Gazza ever worked it out, but it was okay. She made me feel okay 'bout it and he didn't end up gettin' jail time in the end. Steve, everybody goes on about how it ended, but there was this other side of the story, too. When I felt guilty 'bout rattin' out my friend, when I needed money to score, when I got kicked outta my place at the end of the year… she was there. She was always there for me when I needed 'er. Like I said, Steve, she could be a class act.

Letter 4

In Brief: Midas Conway, 45, has been convicted for the second time of murdering Lisa Richardson. On 18 October 2000, Ms Richardson died of injuries sustained in a frenzied attack by her former fiancé, Midas Conway. When the knife Conway had concealed in his clothes broke during his attack on Ms Richardson, Conway found another knife nearby, with which to complete his attack.

Dear Pete,

Some women, who've experienced domestic violence, throw their stories down like gauntlets. Explicit in detail, unwavering in their gaze, they dare you to cringe with every hoarse syllable. There was a time in my post-Pete life when I was like that, too, but here's the thing...

There's always a moment, after confessing that you once stayed with a man, who abused you. There's a look in the listener's eyes that screams, 'Why didn't you just leave?' Sometimes, there's a quick recovery; a well-intentioned, 'Well done for leaving!' or, even more tragically, the pseudo-empathy, 'That must have been awful.' Some people reach for a flimsy attempt at solidarity, 'My sister was once with a man like that. It took her ten years to leave.'

So, you may find some sense of satisfaction in the fact that you have finally silenced me about our life together. There was a time you warned me never to call the police or concocted some excuse I would tell the neighbours for my latest injury. Well, nowadays, our life is truly a taboo and I dread the day I will have to tell our son about it. I fear he will look at me like all those strangers, demanding an answer, 'Why didn't you just leave?'

The truth is my love for you embarrasses me, now. In your mind, you will put this down to the fact that I'm a stuck-up bitch, who always thought I was too good for you. Trust me, Pete... that has nothing to do with it. I was very young. I kind of got a kick out of the fact that this tough guy, who looked like some meth-dealing biker, with the body of a full-forward, would get nervous before he kissed me.

What in God's name was I thinking? (I considered myself a feminist, for Christ's sake!)

I guess I was not as immune from the 'chick flick' myths of romance as I'd like the think I was (in those movies jealousy is invariably equated with passion, couples 'fight' for their love and good sex is always a knock-down, drag-out affair often involving kitchen benches). Pete, as naïve as the notion seems to me now, I think I quite liked the idea that you and I could be star-crossed lovers. I guess there was something so intoxicatingly seductive about simple, small-town boy meets bourgeois (wanna-be bohemian) city girl that I couldn't resist trying to make 'us' work.

It embarrasses me because I should have seen you coming a mile away. I remember the scotch glass sometimes because that was the first time you hurt me physically. You were very drunk, Pete, but do you remember? Can you remember shoving it coarsely into me, spitting out the word 'cunt' and kind of just staring at me, like you were looking through me? It was, by no means, the first compromise, but it was the first time I let you make love to me after you kissed away my tears.

You may find it strange that, amongst survivors of domestic violence, there is an unspoken injunction against talking about good sex. Graphic details of rape are more palatable than describing tender moments of ecstacy (I guess no one wants to admit they sold their birth-right for a good lay!). But, here's the thing… when you made love to me, you were always in the moment. Perhaps, there is something exhilarating about feeling a man, who has unleashed his fury all over you, touching you with gentleness. When he is driven to tears when he apologises… well, maybe, you can't help but sit up and take notice.

There was something so tender about every time you made love to me, after hurting me. Each time you planted a mellow kiss on my bare

skin, it was like we were turning back pages and starting the story all over again. With your mouth and your cock and those dark expressions, you always knew just what to do or say to silence that part of me that had always known exactly what you were and that there wasn't a thing I could do to change you.

I remember the first recoil when you told me you hated how I dressed. You were tentative, still, practicing your art, but you were a quick learner. When did you figure out that 'slut' didn't hurt me nearly as much as when you called me 'stuck-up'? Did you smell the stench of my middle-class guilt?

It would be so easy if I could blame how you treated me on heroin addiction, Pete, but I have come to realise, that if there hadn't been that excuse, you would have found another one. Towards the end, even my sobriety was offensive, wasn't it?

And, still here I am, years later, writing, begging for it not to be my fault. Wanting the relief of those moments when the regret in your eyes was so tangible it hurt to look at. Maybe you won't believe me, but I still mourn those mornings, when I awoke to see your dark eyes, filled with the promise of new beginnings.

Now, there is a new ritual that shapes my mornings. I wake up early so I can change my clothes two or three times, before leaving for work. I mercilessly hound my sons, Braydon and Michael, at the breakfast table, to comment on what I am wearing. Sometimes, Braydon rolls his eyes at Michael, thinking I can't see.

'Do I look okay? Not too much?' I twirl around and the boys reply mechanically, 'You look fine Mum!'

I know you so well Pete. If you were reading this, you would think that this is just one more example of my vanity, but the truth is I have found it difficult to enter every room since I stopped being a drug addict.

Desperately paranoid that the world will see me as a fraud (a junkie in a professional's clothing), I take extra care with first impressions. When someone comments on my new skirt or shoes, I am pathetically relieved. ('Phew! I have dressed right. Now, my work can speak for itself!').

I mastered this quaint neurosis when I was with you. As a mature-aged student, it was difficult to walk into tutorials filled with young, beautiful adolescents, as my waist thickened from being pregnant with Michael. Growing more visibly pregnant over the months I spent entering those rooms to debate semiotics or gay and lesbian literature, I braced myself for each encounter, taking extra care with what I wore, careful to hide old track marks.

Later, entering criminal law lecture halls, it was the bruises on my face I took care to hide. Sometimes, the effort I take to cloak my shame about loving you is exhausting. I imagine that fact is satisfying to you. Even now, your presence still dominates my mornings. I will do anything to avoid that look that demands an explanation and screams, 'Why didn't you just leave?' So, I take care to dress like a woman, who never would have fallen in love with you.

V

*

Mum always reckoned that things went to shit 'coz o' my drinkun. Maybe she 'ad a point. I mean the first restrainin' order was kinda 'coz o' my drinkun.

What 'appened was that a l'il while after I got with 'er, I went out and got drunk. I asked her to come out with me to the club. She said, 'I can't. I've got my son tomorrow.' Fair enough. She'd made 'er choice.

I got totally blind drunk that night and I admit it… I did some things I regret. That freaky, hippy, old chick, who thought you could use a special salt to cure cancer… fucking her was not me finest moment, but, hey, at the end of the day, she hadda know I only done it 'coz I was maggotted… why was she so pissed off?

She was slammin' the washun up, when I went over the next night. Her son was in bed.

'What's wrong babe?' I knew what it was about. I'm not stupid. She was mad I'd slept with the old hippy chick, who thought salts could cure cancer. I hadda lotta time for Gazza. He was me mate, but he could never keep 'is mouth shut about anythun. He was worse than a fuckin' woman, in that way. I've got no doubt he let slip I fucked the old 'salt cures cancer' hippy.

'What do you think is wrong, Pete?' she asked. She was furious. I played dumb.

'I dunno. Is it time for ya period?'

'Yes! That must be it! I'm furious with you because it's *that* time of the month!' she says, all posh 'n' sarcastic. 'It wouldn't have anything to do with you treating me like a fool.'

'Whatcha goin' on about?'

'Puhlease!' she said, bangin' dishes as she put 'em away. 'By the time I got up the street this morning, your sexual escapades were the joke of the day, Pete!'

'This is 'bout the crazy old chick, who was stayin' next door to Gazza, isn't it?'

'Look, I don't care who you sleep with, but I don't want to be worrying about sexually transmitted diseases. In case you haven't noticed, I've got enough to deal with right now!'

'Well, you don't have to worry.' I looked her straight in the eye-steady as 'n' I lied to 'er,

'Nothin' happened, okay.' She wanted to believe me. I came up behind her and nibbled 'er neck. She started to pull away and I pulled 'er into me arms. 'Really, babe, I'm not lyin'! Yeah, I got pissed with 'er at the club and she crashed at me place, but nothin' 'appened, babe. You know how they are 'round here… Gazza'll start any fuckin' rumour just to make life more interestin'.' I put me arms around her, kissed 'er 'ead, slipped me hands under 'er bra, 'Come on, babe, you know that.'

Two days later, there was a note under me door. I know it's from 'er-same purple paper, neat writin', blue biro:-

It's over, Pete. Please don't come around anymore. Fucking bitch! Why couldn't she ever just take me word for anythin'?

I tried reasonin' with 'er through the screen door. She wasn't gunna let me in.

'Why won't ya believe me, babe?'

'It's not about that, Pete. I've just got to focus on my son, now. He's still so fragile. I'm trying to get him comfortable with being with me again. I can't be in a relationship, right now. I am not ready for anything serious, right now, and things are getting far too intense between us.' Her voice was soft 'n' reasonable, but I knew the bitch was lyin'.

'Who is he?' I asked her.

'Who's who?' She looked confused.

'Who're you fucking? Is it Gazza?' She looked at me, 'er eyes wide. She was mad 'n' offended 'bout that one!

'For Christ's sake! Grow up!' She slammed the door in me face.

I held meself back, Steve. I woulda smashed her door in and broken her face, there and then, but I didn't. I waited hours 'n' hours; stewun, mate. The bitch hadda pay for makun me feel like that. I spent 'ours workin' out what I was gunna say and just 'ow I was gunna say it, then I knocked on 'er door. She opened her door, kept the screen door locked. 'Watch that fucking kidda yours.' That's all I said. I didn't touch 'er. I clenched me teeth, but I didn't raise a finger to 'er.

So, I got drunk, did some things I'm not proud of and, when she broke up with me, I got fuckin' angry, but what was the crazy bitch thinkun gettin' an apprehended violence order (A.V.O)? I mean, mate… who gets a goddamned restrainin' order over somethin' like that?

I ignored her. I kept meself to meself. I stopped wantin' 'er, mate. When I thought about her, I'd wank with a kinda boilin' rage that made the whole thing nasty. So I stopped.

I saw her 'round. The kid was comin' over more often. He was a little ferret-faced dweeb. I heard him talkun a couple of times. He talked posh too.

Then I couldn't help meself. I cornered her, as she was lettin' 'erself into her flat, one afternoon,

'So you gunna take this A.V.O off, or what?'

'I don't know,' she said. She looked me straight in the eye, her mouth set, 'Is my son still in danger?'

'As if I'd hurt a kid! Look, I'm sorry, but I was just tryin' to blow off steam 'coz when you ended it, I was so fucking mad! I wanna be with ya, don't you care 'bout that? What was I to you- just a cheap fuck, so you can brag to your posh uni mates you done a workin' class fella?' She let herself in, locked me out with the screen door. She started talkun in that posh voice she used sometimes when she wanted to lord over you how fucking smart and superior she was.

'Pete, are you *that* delusional?' I clenched me fists in my pockets. I needed to see where she was goin' with this. Her nostrils flared up 'n' then 'er voice got all pissy. 'How can you stand there and portray me as the 'bad guy' in all of this? For Christ's sake, Pete, you threatened my son! You humiliated me! You lied to me and you have the gall to say it's because I used you for sex!' She was cranky, man!

'Again with the crazy old chick?! How many times I gotta tell ya? Nothin' happened!' I had me hands 'gainst the screen door and me nose was 'gainst the mesh. Me voice was pretty loud so maybe I was scarin' her a bit. She looked a bit nervous, 'n' she stepped away from the door a bit, before she started talkun again.

'Look,' she said. Her voice was all posh 'n' reasonable 'n' calm, 'At the end of the day, it doesn't matter if anything happened, Pete. I think we just need to cut our losses. We had some fun, but it didn't work out. Let's just leave it at that.'

'Fine, I'll leave ya alone, but are you gunna take the A.V.O off, or what?' She searched me eyes and then nodded.

I didn't go near 'er. Not until she stood in court and the magistrate asked her if she still wanted the A.V.O and she said 'no'. When he dismissed the application, I went to the pub. I drank outta relief and desperation not to do what I knew I wanted to do. I tried not thinkun 'bout that pussy, while I drank me beers.

But it was always like that with us. She couldn't stay away any more than I could. We were soul mates, I guess.

When I staggered to 'er door that night, I hated meself and I hated her.

She was expectin' me. She musta been. She was wearin' this sexy blue satin robe.

I asked for a glass and skulled a coupla shots of scotch. She wasn't drinkin'. I pulled open 'er robe. She was nude and shakin'.

'Let's see how much this cunt can handle.' I picked up the empty scotch glass and shoved it into her real rough. 'Is that good?' She looked at me; that victim thing happening again, hot tears comin' down 'er cheeks. I was hurtin' 'er and gettun hard *as*, mate.

'Please stop,' she whimpered. I snapped out of it then, pulled out the glass, held 'er in me arms.

'I'm sorry. I thought it was gunna feel good for ya,' I lied. She was bawlin' her eyes out, now, so I held her tight.

She was such a precious bitch. She could suck me off like a hoover, but got all teary over a measly glass.

'Shh, shh,' I whispered. She was shakin' and cryin' real hard now, 'I wanna make love to you, babe. Come on, stop cryin'.' She wiped her eyes and slowly the cryin' stopped. I pulled off her robe.

I was gentle with her that night. I watched her peaceful face, as she slept.

I dunno if you ever been in love, mate. It's terrifyin', man. That night I could feel it. A part of me hated her for makin' me feel like that because, watchun 'er sleep that night, I knew I was ruined. I knew there was nothin' I wouldn't do to be with 'er and that scared me shitless.

*

They brought in a new in-mate, today, Steve. I remembered 'im right away. He used to live at those crappy guvvy flats, where I ended up livin' with 'er at the end. I scored weed off 'im a coupla times and he used to sell speed too. He knew why I was in. Most people know the story. Everyone in 'ere claims they was framed. Everyone in 'ere pretends to believe each other. It'd be kinda funny. Only in my case, it happens to be true.

'Fucking tough break,' he said, 'you know, she fucked me for speed one time when you were still together.'

'You and ev'ry man and his dog, mate,' I said. Me voice was relaxed and we pissed ourselves laughing for a bit. I didn't let on that ev'ry one of these confessions from guys, who'd had a taste of her –and fuck knows! there's been a lot of them- cut through me like a knife.

I did some things when I was boozin', no doubt, but the newspapers painted her as some do-gooder/ angel, you know. Like none of it was ever 'er fault. In the papers, they made out she was this single mum, who'd fallen on hard times and studied hard to be a lawyer so she could *help people*. Help people, my ass! She was a fucking skank and she was crazy and no one, but me, seemed to know it. I knew what the bitch was capable of.

I coulda told me lawyer what a skanky slut she was, I guess, but I don't think it woulda helped. It probably woulda made me look guiltier. It woulda just shown I had a reason to hate her. Those lawyers, you know, they all act like they're part of some cool, special club. And she was one of theirs.

*

It was only a little while, after I started sleepin' with 'er. Me mate Mikey (from school, who played on the first fifteen with me- remember him?) invited me to go fishin' with him 'n' 'is new bitch. I took off; didn't tell her I was goin'. Maybe, that's why she thought she had the right to do what she did.

He was me best mate, for fuck's sake! That weekend, she felt dumped. That's the only way I can explain it.

And Gazza, he was me mate, but he was a manipulative prick 'n' 'e was always runnin' a scam. You could see the gullibility in her eyes just lookin' at 'er. Because she was smart, but she was book smart. She didn't get that she was beautiful, so all you hadda do was tell her she was gorgeous and the stupid bitch would fall all over herself thankin' you.

I think that's how it happened. He rocked up with tequila (tequila, for fuck's sake!). He'd probably swiped it from the supermarket and that was the thing about that Gazza. He was a born con-man. He hadda trade that tequila for somethin'. It was in 'is nature. He wanted her, he was jealous of me and somehow, he hadda get her to think it was okay.

I knew the moment I got back. Gazza was like burstin' to tell. Like I said, mate, Gazza could never keep 'is mouth shut 'bout anythin'. In the end, he tried to look all sorry,

'Mate, better you hear it from me, you know. I'll understand if you wanna belt the shit out of me, Lloydee...' The way he explained it blew me away; like he'd done it to test her, ya know, to see if she was gunna be faithful to me. Yeah, right! I let it go. Plus, Gazza was built like a fucking brick shit-house. I didn't know if she was worth it.

'I'm not gunna hit you Gazza, but I've gotta get away from you for a bit, right now, mate.' He moved away, didn't yell or anythin' when I slammed his door shut so hard I split the wood.

I went straight over to 'er place. She was cryin', when she told me.

'I'll only talk about this once. I won't talk about it again. I regret what I did and I still can't understand how it happened, but it did. Pete, I will tell you the story because I *am* sorry and I owe you an explanation, but I'm not going to live with you constantly throwing this back in my face.' She stopped, gulped, took a breath, went on. She started talkun real staunchly, 'I will promise you now nothing like this will ever happen again.' She stopped 'n' looked me dead in the eye. 'But you need to promise me that we can move on from this or you can walk out that door, now, and never come back.' She stopped, looked at me 'ard, waited for me to agree. I nodded, me teeth clenched. She couldn't look at me.

Her eyes were cold and she stared straight ahead at the wall 'n' started talkun real softly.

'He came over with a bottle of tequila and I told him I didn't feel like drinking- maybe later,' she said. The tears were runnin' down her face now. Her voice was filled with shame and her voice kept breakun as she told the story. I almost felt sorry for 'er.

54

'I could tell that he wanted me. But here's the thing, Pete, he's not even my type and, yes, I was flattered, but there was no way I was going to have sex with him ... Then, I don't know how it happened, but we ended up drinking tequila shots and I got pretty wasted. I still can't understand how. I think I only drank a shot or two and alcohol's never affected me like that before, but, then again, I've never really been a drinker...' She stopped, looked at 'er hands, then started talkun again. 'When I came to, he was on top of me. I regretted it as soon as it was over. He didn't know what was wrong. He looked so confused. I asked him to leave. He picked up his box of condoms and the rest of his tequila and left.' She was shakin', now, as she bawled her eyes out. I didn't give a shit.

I put me hands on the back of her 'ead- one on each side- and shoved me cock in her mouth, after that. I'd never done it with 'er like that before 'coz she'd told me she hated it- right at the start when I first got with 'er. So, I knew she hated ev'ry minute of it, but she deserved it that night. She knew it. She didn't get precious about it, so I knew she could tell she deserved it. She was red-eyed and gaggin' when I'd finished with 'er. I felt sick to me stomach when I looked at her.

'I can't stand to look at you right now. Get your clothes on and get out,' I said. I was so angry. I needed to get her away from me or I was gunna kill 'er. The stupid bitch grinned,

'This is my house.' I faced 'er squarely.

'Not right now, bitch. Get the fuck out!' She knew I meant it and she crawled outta there fucking smartly. I locked 'er out. I dunno where she slept that night and I don't care.

Me point is this. She wasn't all fucking sweetness and light. I loved her. I love her still, but it's like you said, Steve, 'The bitch was bad news.'

55

Gazza and I were okay, after a while. I owed 'im a fair bitta money for pot. He wiped me dope debt. We had a few beers together. He shouted me a coupla sticks of weed. We never talked 'bout it again.

A few weeks later, Gazza bragged to another mate that he'd spiked her drink with some pretty heavy duty shit. The story got back to me, but I never did tell 'er. The slut deserved to feel fucking dirty and guilty.

Letter 5

Local News, 15 November 2000

Yesterday, a thirty-five year old man and a twenty-nine year old woman were found in the lounge room of their house on a remote property near Goondiwindi, 500 kilometres south-west of Brisbane. Both had gunshot wounds to the head. Police took about twenty minutes to reach the property, after receiving a Triple 0 call from a man claiming to have shot his wife. Police noted that the couple had a history of domestic violence.

Dear Pete,

I *don't know if you've kept up, but I work with victims, now. In my practice, I make a point of telling women that violence is never okay. Domestic violence is always an abuse of human rights. Still, I can't help but recognise the familiar flickering in their eyes sometimes... Other professionals see ambivalence, where I see guilt.*

It seems silly to me to be writing this apologia- seeing as you'll never read it- but there is something more irresistible than therapy about these pre-drawn writing sessions. And here's the thing, Pete... you may not believe this, but I still agonise over my part in it all. When I give in to the guilt, I can see my twenty-something-year-old self the way you must have. I was a shameless flirt! Lustful male glances were still a novelty in my twenties and I savoured them.

Maybe, a part of me enjoyed toying with your jealousy, too. It's no excuse, but I was very young, Pete. In retrospect, I wish that the twenty-something girl, who loved feeling sexy, was a little more frigid. Perhaps my vanity made me fair game for a predator like Gazza with his tequila. Locked out of my flat that night, I sat on a swing in one of the local parks, aimlessly swinging back and forth, watching passing traffic, sleeplessly embracing the cold and thinking it was a fitting punishment for my betrayal. After all, a more modest woman wouldn't have been taken in by Gazza.

With years of practice and distance, I am supposed to have internalised rebuttals for these rationalisations for your violence. After all, I have represented women, who made my singlets (the ones you thought were slutty) seem demure. I would never question their right to be safe from violence. I have spent eons rehearsing positive self-talk to counter my negative thoughts and, sometimes, it works, but, more often than not, I have to confess the practice of talking back to my thoughts still feels unnatural and the self-loathing has an authenticity that the therapeutic self-talk never will.

It will please you to know that the girl who liked to feel sexy is long gone. My fondness for fucking has faded with time, too. Now, desiring male glances unsettle me. Sometimes I feel a little queasy, my hands feel clammy and male advances raise the hairs on the back of my neck. It is as if my skin has internalised all your accusations.

After Gazza, I felt like I owed you some lee-way, so it was a long time before I resented you for accusing me of infidelities that only existed in your mind. And, Pete, here I am, years later, wondering if a more wholesome version of me would have kept your jealous rages in check.

Other guilty doubts that keep me awake before dawn are even harder to quash. I often wonder whether things could have been different if I had told you Michael was your child from the start. I remember the night I finally told you- how carefully I worded my explanation for lying to you and how incomplete it was...

It all started with two pink lines. I was quickly consumed with a strange, petty anger; furious, beyond reason, at the fact that pregnancy test manufacturers thought pink was a fitting colour.

I can still recall those seething thoughts word-for-word, Pete. In my mind, I fumed,

'There are things that are supposed to be pink! This isn't one of them! Strawberry yogurt should be pink! Satin brides-maid's dresses- sleeveless, corseted and full-skirted- they can be pink! Fairy floss should never be anything but pink! Lines that appear when you have a pregnancy test that's positive should not be fucking pink!' (It's true, when

you think about it. Pink is a trivial colour. The two lines that change your life forever really shouldn't be pink.)

After the ranting, internal diatribe was complete, I froze. Then, the panic articulated itself very inelegantly and not very eloquently. Sitting on the toilet, panties at my ankles, dribbles of urine still dripping into the water in the toilet bowl, the plastic test in my hand, I said, simply, out loud, into the empty bathroom, 'Shit!

I sat on that toilet seat for the longest time, holding that silly bit of plastic still wet from my urine (Honestly! Could they make the process of finding out you're pregnant any more mortifying?). The thought that entered my mind was crudely succinct. 'What the fuck am I going to do?'

You may find this hard to believe, but, even then, when we had been together for such a short time, the fear burrowed quietly in my gut incessantly. When I found out I was pregnant, it came to the surface and washed over me with the starkness of irrefutable fact. Your violence was going to escalate.

I was becoming adept at denial by then, so I was accustomed to silencing that inner voice that told me to get away from you as fast as I could. Now, suddenly, there were two of us you could hurt and that inner voice was a roar.

The grim calculations began circling in my mind. If I went to a refuge, Richard would balk at Braydon spending time with me, there. How would I explain to him that I'd mucked things up for Braydon all over again?

There was no way I could move back home. The doubt in my mother's eyes after my two stabs at heroin addiction still lingers, even now. She can never quite believe I'm not going to preface each conversation, with some elaborately manufactured story about why I need to borrow some cash from her (which I will spend on my next hit, like I used to in the old days). I watch the tension in her back dissipate when she walks away from me, even these days. She is relieved that there's a chance she might be able to trust me again.

When I think about how I came to a solution to my dilemma, I feel absurd, but I have learnt, over the years, that desperation makes for the most unfortunate of decisions. Reading voraciously that spring was helping to stave off the persistent clamour. If I became engrossed in a good book, the urge to score was somewhat sated.

One afternoon, reading to keep the panic at bay, I found my answer in Colleen McCullough's Thorn Birds. *Like Meggie, I would lie about my child's paternity. I would offer you the option of walking away from the 'shit-house, junkie Mum' (your words, Pete, not mine), who was pregnant with another man's child. If you took it, then I'd be safe and so would my baby.*

I regret that decision every day, Pete. If I had been honest with you from the start, maybe you would have seen how much I loved you and everything might have been different...

It was true what I told you that night, when I finally confessed. I really did sense that you weren't ready to be a father, but maybe that wasn't my choice to make for you. I'm sorry for the time you missed out on looking forward to our child because of my lie.

Maybe, I sold you short when it came to Braydon, too. I was always so careful to take responsibility for a child that wasn't yours. Perhaps I pushed you away.

But, in my defence, when Braydon came to live with me, the arrangement felt so tenuous... Do you know that I have hoarded every single playgroup flyer, from that time? They are still packed in a box in the

garage and I still have the copious photos I took of Braydon on swings and slides at the parks we visited.

And this'll sound crazy, but I still have every bus ticket from those two-hour return bus trips. I kind of cherish the fact that I spent a lot of time catching buses to get Braydon to child-care. You thought it was silly and that I should have enrolled him in child-care in town, but Pete, I felt like I owed Braydon the security of not changing child-care centres. He had started child-care in the city, while I was A.W.O.L. as his mother. On probation as a parent, I hesitated to change anything about Braydon's routine. I put up with the burden of many bus trips to make sure that as little as possible changed for my son, when he came to live with me.

Sometimes when the doubts are hollering within me, I finger these tokens. When I hold fading bus tickets, I know I was willing to sit on many buses to prove (to Richard or his mother or to myself- I'm not sure whom...) that I could be a 'good' mother and put Braydon first.

And, Pete, although I did not tell you I was pregnant with your child, at first, this much is true: there wasn't a second I contemplated aborting your child. I dreamt of a child with your dark eyes and goofy grin. Would that admission have made all the difference, Pete? I can't help, but wonder...

V

*

In spite of her faults, when I think back on it, I reckon we woulda been all right- if there were no kids. But she loved that friggun kid. And I couldn't stand him!

I'm rememberin' 'er on the phone, to the kid's grandmother pretty early on in the piece, when they agreed the kid was gunna come back 'n' live with 'er. She's got her posh voice on and she says,

'Sarah, I can understand why you would be reluctant to consider this … but I promise you I'm not going to put Braydon in that situation. That's why I went back on the methadone programme. I'm off methadone, now, Sarah, but I have asked my doctor to put me on random urine tests every week because I don't want any wriggle room. If one of those tests comes back positive, you could use it against me in court, we both know that! I'm putting myself in that position because, if I start using heroin again, *I actually don't want him around, okay*?'

She sounded like she was in a debate team or somethin', as she tried to persuade the hag on the other end of the line she was clean and gunna stay that way. I was sittin' in the livin' room watchin' her standun in the kitchen on the phone. Her back was tense. She'd asked me to be quiet and I just wanted her to hurry up, so I could fuck 'er. Much more of this drivel and I was gunna lose me hard-on.

She was listenin' real hard now.

'Absolutely! But we'll try it and see how it goes?' Her voice was all keen, mate. She sighed. Big sigh of relief, her shoulders relaxed. 'Okay. Thank you! Thank you! You won't regret it, I promise!' She hung up the phone. She was fucking beamin'. It was the first real smile I'd ever seen.

She bounced- yeah, bounced!- onto the sofa.

'Braydon's coming back to live with me! I've got to stay clean, of course, but he's going to come and stay with me two days a week, then three days a week, until he's living here!' She was so stoked, mate, but I just couldn't fake it. It was gunna to be a nightmare. I was gettin' softer by the second.

'After everythun these people done to you,' I said real slowly. She'd told me about how they crucified her in court for bein' a junkie, 'how can you be so fucking nice? That woman took your son away, from you, damn it! Why don't ya just make a clean break? Wouldn't it be easier? He can live with his Dad and his Gran. You never have to deal with 'em again. I'm just thinkin' of you, babe. I've seen this tear ya apart.'

The glow in her face was gone just like that. She looked kinda blown away.

'This is my son,' she said, 'You understand what that means, right? We're a package deal, Pete. I can't *not* be with my son.' I pulled her into me arms.

'Yeah, yeah, I get it. It's just gunna take some gettin' used to.' She was so small, so flimsy in me arms. I kissed the top of her head, 'A little gettin' used to, that's all...'

I said the words, but I didn't believe 'em. I was right. It was a fucking nightmare!

But then again, Steve, everything was complicated with that chick. She musta known I wasn't ready to be a father. That's why she had that talk with me, when she told me she was pregnant. She wasn't even showin' yet when she told me. She had 'er posh, lord it over you voice on again. She said what she hadda say real matter of fact 'n' a bit abrupt like she wasn't gunna enter into any discussion 'bout it-no matter what I hadda say.

'Pete, I've calculated the dates. It isn't yours. You need not worry about that and I'll understand if you don't want to be with me anymore, but I can't kill this child. I don't think it's in me to have an abortion.'

'Well, what d'ya expect from me?' I asked 'er. Her voice was casual, then.

'Nothing. We're having fun, we have good sex, we're not hurting anyone, why does there have to be anything else?' You know, mate, I had no good answer for that one. Why couldn't we just keep fucking? I shoulda taken her up on 'er offer. I know that now, but I can be a stupid prick, mate. Sometimes, I cut me nose off to spite me face.

'What if I want somethin' more, babe?' She looked real uncomfortable, then. It took a long time for her to start talkun again.

'Then, it's like this, Pete. You take me as I am.' She looked me dead in the eye. 'Lord knows, I've got regrets and I know I'm not perfect, but if you want to be part of my life, you accept me and my children and you make a commitment to treat us well. If you can't do that, we can keep seeing each other, but you'll have to accept I have a life apart from you.' I got what she was sayin'. If I was gunna be with 'er, I was always gunna be second to 'er kids. You're me brother, Steve. The one thing you gotta know about me, by now, is I don't like havin' the law laid down and I hate the stuck-up bitches that lord it over you when they do it.

'I'll have to think 'bout it.'

'Take all the time you need, Pete.'

At first, I tried sneakin' in to fuck her after her son was asleep. I'd try 'n' be gone before he was awake. One mornin', he found us in the livin' room on the sofa bed, tangled together under the sheets.

'Go, get dressed, sweetie. I'll just be a minute,' she said, half-asleep. I was wide awake in an instant.

'Fuck!' I said, under me breath, when he was outta the room.

'What's wrong?' she asked, as she got busy dressin'.

'What do you mean, what's wrong? This is not fair on 'im! His mother is sleepun with some strange fella in the livin' room.' She totally didn't get it. She just smiled 'n' said,

'Calm down Pete! It's all right, really. I'll just explain to Braydon that Mummy had a sleepover, that's all. You might want to be more careful about setting the alarm next time, Pete.' She kissed me quick on the lips as she finished dressin'. 'Lock the door on your way out.' Stupid bitch! I got dressed and got outta there. She could be so fucking stupid!

I tried to stay, away, when I could see her son was 'round. Then, I cottoned on. The dopey bitch needed me. It was like I said to you, mate, she just had no idea 'bout the world she was livin' in now.

'Twas just before Christmas, when Gazza's seedy mate, Smithy, dropped by to see me 'n' 'e was desperate. She was cookin' up a batch of stroganoff 'coz I'd told 'er 'twas my favourite 'n' 'twas one of our few nights together, without that fuckin' dweeby kid of hers around. He was at his Gran's. Smithy'd brought over a heapa toys 'n' a stick of pot to share. I was choppin' it up to pack it into cones, like ya do.

'Look, I can't find the receipts 'n' my son's not comin' up for Christmas now. I've gotta pay my electicity, mate, so I thought your missus might be interested,' he says. Look, I knew the toys were hot, but I couldn't say anythin' 'coz otherwise he was gunna fuck off with 'is dope. For fuck's sake, she shoulda cottoned on!

'Babe, are ya interested?' I called out. She came outta the kitchen, lickin' sour cream off a wooden spoon.

'Interested in what?' she asked. Smithy gave 'er 'is pitch. He had the look down pat too. He looked like a man 'shamed that he was in such a tight spot 'n' desperate to get out of it. He played it just right and the stupid bitch fell for it.

'I've got these toys 'coz my son was meant to come down this Christmas. My psycho ex has changed her mind. I can't find receipts so I can't get a refund and I've got this killer electricity bill, so I need the money and I'm willing to fire-sale the stuff so my power doesn't get cut off. I thought you might be able to use them.' She was supposed to piss in 'is pocket for a bit, while I got a coupla cones into me. For fuck's sake! She'd been a junkie, why didn't she cotton on?

'They're not stolen, are they?' she asked. Stupid bitch! Like, he was gunna say, 'Yeah, actually...'

'No way! Like I said, I'm just in a tight spot 'coz of my psycho ex.' She went back into the kitchen, pottered 'round on the stove for a bit, then came back out.

'Okay,' she said, 'I'll have a look.'

Steve, she loved that kid. I could see it in 'er eyes. She coulda never afforded to give 'im the Christmas she wanted to or that he was gunna get with his dad 'n' Gran. She saw those toys 'n' she saw a way to make Christmas special.

68

'How much?' she asked 'n' I knew it'd gone too far. I shoulda pulled 'er into the bed-room 'n' told 'er what was goin' on. I couldn't. Smithy's stick was the only way I was gunna get to smoke any pot that day. I was suckin' down as many cones as I could, while they haggled over the price 'coz I knew Smithy'd be outta there as soon as the deal was done 'n' he was too much of a player to leave any dope behind, but, mate, the chick was supposed to be smart! How could she *not* get what was goin' on?

She put me in a tricky position. She was stoked that she'd made such a good deal. I couldn't tell 'er what I knew 'bout Smithy, 'coz then she'd rip into me 'bout not stoppin' her, ya know. I hadda keep me mouth shut. I hadda listen to 'er ravin' on and on 'bout 'ow happy she was she could give Braydon a proper Christmas 'n' bite me fucking tongue. Fucking dopey bitch!

When she came home after bein' arrested, she was devastated. The cops'd taken all the Christmas presents; even the ones that were legit!

'It was pathetic, Pete. I was just sitting in the back seat of the police car, crying my eyes out. What am I going to do?'

I gave 'er the name of the lawyer, who got me off when Mum'd charged me with assault. She started budgetin' manically 'n' livin' on two-minute noodles. Later on in the piece, she did some voluntary hours of community service with the Salvation Army and she got off the receivin' stolen goods charges.

The night before Christmas, she'd gotten together a coupla decent Christmas presents. I didn't see 'is face when 'e opened them, but she was beamin' when she told me 'bout it after, so I guess her kid wasn't disappointed.

I felt like I owed 'er then, I guess. Plus, I was about to get evicted. That's why I told 'er what I did that Sundee night ('twas New Year's

Eve, but we were both too broke to go out-Christmas'd wiped 'er out 'n' I'd spent all my cash on pot as usual). After we'd made love, I said,

'I want it to be more than just fucking.' She looked at me hard.

'Are you sure?' I kissed her head. She was lyin' on me chest.

'Yeah, I'm sure.'

*

Our life together was a buncha chores after I moved in. Her faggotty kid was livin' with us. She'd walk up the street to get her bread 'n' milk. She'd come back and catch two buses to take 'im to day-care. She'd catch two buses back. By the time she finished washun clothes 'n' she'd had somethin' to eat 'n' cleaned up the place a bit, it was time for her to catch the bus to pick up 'er son again.

She was startin' to get a fair way along by then and ev'ry night she looked exhausted. A part of me felt sorry for 'er, mate, but another parta me couldn't even go there. She was tired 'coz she was knocked up with another fella's baby. If I got meself thinkin' along those lines, I didn't know what I'd do, so I just didn't go there…

*

I dunno what possessed me to ask 'er, in the end, but I did. I guess I just hadda know, mate. She'd got the kid off to bed and she looked wrecked. She was too tired to get into pyjamas and she was sittun there in 'er maternity jeans and a nice pink top she used to wear. She could hardly keep 'er eyes open.

'Is there any chance it's mine?' I asked 'er and, like that, she was awake. I knew what she was gunna say before she said it. She squirmed. Looked at her hands for a bit, sat on 'em, finally, looked me in the eye. She had her posh voice on again. She couldn't help it- the freaky bitch. She hadda lord it over me, while she confessed.

'When I found out the pill hadn't worked and I was pregnant, Pete, I was shell-shocked. You see, I had plans for this year. I got myself off methadone so I could go back to university. Plus, I knew you weren't ready to be a father, Pete. There were a million perfectly logical reasons *not* to have this child.' She stopped for a bit, cleared her throat and then went on,

'But try to understand, Pete, I know what it's like to lose a child,' she said. She stopped, looked down at 'er hands again, 'When that Family Court judge said I could only have contact with Braydon at his child-care centre and that he couldn't live with me, it was like losing a child, like they'd torn him out of me. It was too much. For a long time, I didn't know how I'd go on.' I could see the memory in 'er face, for just a second. Then, she gotta hold of herself. Her eyes looked cold and dead. She couldn't even go there 'n' feel *it* again, Steve. It was *that* painful for 'er.

She stopped again, took a breath. 'It got better with time, but it was always there. Sometimes, that feeling of loss was really faint, just like a whisper, but other times, I could feel it in every inch of my body like a scream.' She trembled for a minute. She looked shattered; then, she looked me in the eye. 'Some days, that feeling of loss overwhelms me. I feel it in every part of my body and it's actually physically painful.' She stopped, like she was rememberin' somethin'.

'Do you remember that first night I came over to your place… and you didn't take advantage of me?' I remembered the taste of her nipples in me mouth, when I'd sucked 'er tits, while she was passed out on me sofa. I nodded and she went on. 'Well, it was one of the days when the loss was a scream. I'd been to the pub and scored some smack in the city, before I came to see you.'

She stopped for a bit. Like the confession'd drained 'er. I didn't know why. It'd been pretty obvious –to me- she'd been wasted on somethin' or other (most likely smack) that night.

She went on. Her eyes were red raw. She hadn't been cryin', but she looked like she had. It took 'er a while to get talkun again.

'When I found out I was pregnant, there were a million good reasons to terminate, but I didn't think I could survive losing another child. I knew if I told you, one of two things would happen, Pete: you'd want me to have an abortion or you'd feel trapped into staying with me. I didn't want to put you in either of those positions. I knew there was no way I could abort a child, so I'm sorry, Pete, but it just seemed fairer to lie to you.' She stopped. The shame on 'er face was clear, but when she started talkun again, she sounded real staunch, 'Look, I don't expect anything from you. I made this choice. I don't expect you to take responsibility for it, when I didn't even consult you about it. I've resigned myself to raising this child alone- without a father- so I don't expect a thing from you, okay?'

I was gutted. I was gunna be a father. I saw that stomach I'd been resistin' punchin' the shit out of for ages in a whole new way. That was *my* child I coulda killed… I was too blown away and sad to be angry at 'er. Me voice sounded far away and soft when I spoke.

'Can I meet it- you know- without lettin' it know who I am?'

'Of course,' she said. Her face was soft with guilt. 'I'm *so* sorry.'

When I told Mum later, she was so incredibly stoked. Her face lit up for the first time in ages. I couldn't just walk away. I couldn't be a hands-off dad. Mum woulda never've accepted it. You've got kids, Steve. You know what she's like with her grandkiddies, mate.

72

'Mum hugged me when I told her,' I said. She was far enough along by then that she was kind of just wrapped up with 'erself and this baby growin' inside 'er. She didn't get how important what I'd just said was. She didn't react. 'You know, it was the first time in ages…'

She was still in her own little world; not listenin', so I decided to wake 'er up.

'I wanna be a dad to this baby,' I said. That fucking snapped her out of it! She looked at me. She was stunned, mate. She'd never really thought this through. She never thought I had rights, but I did. It was time to claim 'em.

'Okay, but you know you don't have to…' She looked terrified.

'I know, but it's my kid.' I didn't say anythin' else. Just that: 'It's my kid.' The words'd been said and they somehow just hung there in the air. She looked confused. 'It *is* mine, isn't it?' She was too shocked to even be offended. Steve, that's how I knew, without a doubt, the kid was mine.

'Well, yes, but…'

'Then I'm gunna be a dad to it.'

I'll never forget 'er face, mate. It had ripped 'er apart to tell me the kid was mine. Now she knew and I knew. There was somethin' more I could take from 'er and she was scared shitless.

Letter 6

In Brief: Ginter Osman (a.k.a. 'Gerry') Mehmet was today jailed for at least thirteen years for the murder of his wife, Vanora. Mehmet, a transport manager, stabbed his wife seven times in their Horsley Park home on April 21, 2001. Judge Virginia Bell noted that, prior to the murder, Mehmet had told members of his wife's family, 'Watch my eyes. If they get big, I am going to kill her.'

ch inside_Updated.indd 75

3/31/2012 7:24:21 PM

Dear Pete,

I have little time for fiction in my post-Pete life, but there are some subjects I find myself reading about voraciously. The way a baby's brain develops in an environment of rage and fear is a subject I've become somewhat of an expert about. Scholarly articles about the impact of domestic violence on children are book-marked on my computer.

I am vigilant for signs. When six-year-old Michael was diagnosed with attention deficit hyperactivity disorder, the paediatrician read my guilt as academic curiosity and used lots of jargon in his reply to my question,

'Is there any chance it could be genetic?'

The morning I had to give my son his first dose of dexamphetamines sent me grappling urgently for the bathroom, where I could weep without my son hearing me...

For a while, Braydon's drawing skills lagged behind those of his peers. I was relieved when the dark stick figures evolved into pastel-coloured snow-men and gratified the first time a tree actually looked like a tree.

An agnostic now (my faith in God another casualty of our time together), I am nonetheless grateful for my children's resilience. Michael still stops and starts a little when he reads picture books he is getting too old for, but I am heartened when he breezes through Dr. Seuss' Green Eggs and Ham. I have less of a love-hate relationship with those morning pills now.

Pete, I confess I have always wanted to ask you and, now, sadly, these letters are my only forum. I tried so hard to understand it at the time (when I was not denying it!). Why did you hate Braydon so much?

I've searched the photos of the little boy I adored so much I could not stop photographing him and I wonder what it is that you saw in him, that inspired such rage... Was it the same thing that you saw in that photo of me with my uni mates? That I had the audacity to have a life before you- why did that scare you so much? It didn't mean I was destined to leave you, Pete. You're the one who set that outcome in motion.

Looking back on my part, I tell myself that I always believed you would fall in love with Braydon eventually; that (with time) you wouldn't be able to resist. Was that naïve of me?

Although I took countless photographs of my son that autumn, I have only one photograph of myself from the time I was pregnant with Michael. I hesitated to ask you to photograph me; fearing my pregnant belly would remind you of my deceit and that that would be enough to set you off.

In the photo, I am standing beside Braydon. We are both wearing pyjamas and holding french fries. We are laughing. When I look at the photo, I remember politely asking a passer-by to take a photo of my son and me, dressed in our pyjamas. I juggled my french fries, as I handed him my camera. When the photographer told us to say, 'Cheese!', I laughed, a little self-consciously and Braydon laughed in that way all kids do, when they are asked to do something silly.

It relieves me that, when I have asked Braydon about living with us in those flats before Michael was born, he tells me he remembers only two things- Pyjama Friday and the Christmas cone.

Do you remember the Christmas cone, Pete? After the police confiscated everything, I could not afford another tree so I bought sheets of card-board and gold wrapping paper and made a Christmas cone. Braydon and I spent a morning in December sticking candy canes on it with sticky-tape for decoration and, on Christmas morning, Braydon woke up to find presents around the cone. He remembers that cone with such a wistful expression that I am grateful I went to the trouble.

Maybe, if you'd seen his face light up that Christmas morning, you would have seen what I saw in my son and why I could never abandon him again.

'You were right, Mummy! I think Santa did find us easy because we were the only ones with a Christmas cone!' I can see his eyes sparkling even now and it pains me to remember when my son started lying to me by omission. He's nearly twelve now and skilled at it (not telling me he has homework doesn't count as lying, in his mind), but that's normal, I'm told. It wasn't normal when he was three.

V

*

In April 2001, she was two and a half months away from givin' birth to our kid. The ultrasound chick had told 'er she was havin' a girl.

The way it started out was that I felt sorry for 'er. She'd go up the street with Braydon. He was gettun too big for a stroller so it'd take 'er ages; then she'd be rushin' 'round, when she got back to get 'im ready for day-care 'n' get 'erself ready for uni if it was one of 'er uni days, ya know. So, I thought I'd be nice 'n' I said,

'Why don't you leave 'im here, while ya go up to the clinic to get ya urines done? It'll make the walk faster for you.'

'Are you sure?'

'Yeah, we'll be right for a bit.'

So, she started leavin' 'im, while she went to get 'er urines done or went up the street for bread 'n' milk.

Well, one time I was a bit hung-over, 'n' kinda just chillun on the sofa, when Braydon says, in 'is posh, dweeby voice,

'Pete, I'm hungry.'

'Your Mum'll be back soon.'

'When?' Every fuckin' whiney word outta the kid's mouth was like a hammer in me head, so maybe I got a bit louder than I shoulda.

'When she gets back! Just shut the fuck up, will ya?'

When she got back the kid was mopin'.

'What's wrong?'

'Nothing,' he mumbles. He looked at me, like he was sealin' a deal. She couldn't see it, but that kid was a fuckin' sneak.

She didn't understand 'bout disciplinin' kids. Look, Steve, to be fair, I don't think she was raised the way we were. Mum was by herself with us three boys. She couldn't pussy-foot around. It was different for her. She was raised richie-rich, you know, and you and me both *know* the rich're different.

I can still remember comin' back on a Saturdee afternoon, after puttin' me footy bets on. I think she was seven months gone, by then. Her son was gettin' picked up by 'is Gran on Saturdee mornin's so 'e was gone.

She shoulda been white. She wasn't. Her voice was pretty calm, pretty casual. The one sign that somethin' was wrong was that she couldn't look at me and I could see her shoulders were tight as. She was washun dishes, when I got there. She kept 'er back to me, while she talked. She never talked without lookin' at ya, so I knew somethin' was off.

'Sarah was furious today,' she said. Sarah was her son's grandmother. I pretended to be interested.

'Yeah? And?'

'She says Braydon has been telling her some of the things you say to him, while I leave him with you in the mornings to go to the clinic for my urines or to the shops to buy bread and milk.' I froze for a minute, but I forced meself not to say a word. She waited. 'He told her you scream and swear at him.' I didn't say a word, while she waited again. Then she turned 'round, looked me dead in the eyes.

'Is it true?' Her eyes were murderous. There was gunna be no way she was gunna let this one go. I hadda think fast mate.

'That kid plays you!' I said all huffy.

'What do you mean, Pete?'

'He knows ya feel guilty 'bout the past so 'e plays you!'

'So you don't scream and swear at him, while I'm at the clinic getting my urines or at the shops buying bread and milk?' Her voice was posh 'n' slow and ev'ry word was careful, 'That's what you're telling me, Pete?'

'Yeah.' I looked her dead in the eye to make the point. She relaxed, then looked away 'n' started thinkin' 'n' talkun - almost to 'erself.

'Okay, well, I guess I'd better have a talk with him. I need to reassure him that, just because you're living here, doesn't mean I love him any less and that he can always come to me, with anything.' She sighed, got back to the dishes.

I'm not a prick. I hadda tell 'er the truth, mate. I wouldna been able to live with meself, if I hadn't. I waited until after we'd made love that night.

'Braydon was tellin' the truth.' I felt her go stiff 'gainst me and I held her tight before she could bolt outta bed. We were lyin' together, spoonin' and I held 'er firm. Somethin' told me I needed to do this *just* right, so I was slow 'n' careful, when I spoke, thinkun 'bout ev'ry word before I said it. 'I know it was wrong and it'll never happen again, babe, but he frustrates me so much, sometimes!' I stopped, focused on soundin' sorry. It came out just right. 'Will you forgive me, babe?'

She was quiet for a while, calculatun. I think she understood, by then, that single motherhood wasn't as cool and romantic as she'd first thought it was gunna be.

'Thanks for telling me,' she said, her body relaxing in me arms. She sighed heavily, 'we're going to get through this.'

We lay in silence for a while and I thought 'bout how easy it'd been. A l'il while ago, she'd tried to lay down the law 'bout treating her 'n' her children well. I'd just crossed the line and she was still lyin' here. She could talk the talk, but she couldn't walk the walk, Steve. It was handy to know…

She started takin' 'er son with 'er everywhere. He was never alone with me. It was exhaustin' for her, I know, but she turned their morning walks into adventures. One day, they walked up the street real early in pyjamas and called it their 'Pyjama Fridee'. Another day they had 'Hippy Tuesdee' and dressed as hippies with bandannas 'n' tie-dyed outfits. She bought 'im a pirate hat and some days they'd walk up the street, speakun in pirate accents. She started makun special times for 'em to 'ave picnic dinners together at the lake. They fed the ducks stale bread; just her 'n' him. I didn't think I had the right to kick up a stink. Besides, at the end of the day, when she fuckin' made the effort, mate, she could be a brilliant Mum.

83

Letter 7

Local News, 18 June 2001

In the Queensland Supreme Court, Peter John Sellick today faced two counts of murder. Mr. Sellick's ex-girlfriend, Anita Harrold, alleged that he punched her in the head, face and breasts, before smashing her head against a car dashboard. Ms Harrold was twenty-two weeks pregnant at the time and lost the twins she was carrying. During the coronial inquest, Ms Harrold said there had been several domestic violence orders taken out against Mr. Sellick.

Dear Pete,

*P*erforming in a court room is all about observation. Getting a feel for the magistrate's mood helps a good solicitor to know when to ask for an adjournment. Taking the time to watch how a defendant reacts to a line of questioning can make or break a cross-examination. So, I spend a lot of time, these days, observing perpetrators of violence. There are patterns amongst the diverse members of this club. Even the obscenely wealthy have nostrils that flare and jaws that clench brutishly. Maybe I have become cynical, but, to me, reactions to hints of female independence seem predictably universal amongst men, who abuse women.

Finishing all my arts units in June meant I could go back to finish the law units of my combined Arts/Law degree the following year. Did that frighten you, Pete?

I have no doubt you got tired of hearing about the last essay I wrote to pass my last Women's Studies unit. But, here's the thing... it wasn't just an essay to me, Pete.

At the risk of sounding conceited, I have to say, it was my piece-de-resistance. I developed a unique thesis, historicising 'heroin chic' as a potent metaphor for Gen-X's disaffection with the scarcity of societal taboos left to break. With that essay, I set out to bury the nostalgic feelings I had harboured for heroin.

Heavily pregnant with Michael, exhausted from studying texts on semiotics and formulating my radical argument, I decided to grow up (as harsh as that sounds) and become someone else, when I wrote that

87

essay. I only have the revised version of that essay now (why did you do it, Pete? I never asked you and, now, on these safe pages, I can. What the hell was so intimidating about my fifteen pages of pain-stakingly crafted double-spaced text that you had to destroy them?).

I never told you where I was when the contractions started. I was sighing with relief, reading my grade, when I anxiously retrieved my marked essay from the faculty office. This will not interest you in the least, but my tutor gave me a high distinction.

Although you may not believe me, I do not begrudge you for those hours I spent alone, in hospital, in early labour. You forget, Pete, I was an addict once, too. I remember the tyranny of addiction well enough to appreciate that there was no way you could face me giving birth without a few cones. So, when I rang you and breathlessly told you I was going into labour, getting to the hospital was a secondary priority to scoring a stick of pot. Although I hated you (at the time) for abandoning me with that annoyingly upbeat midwife, full of pep talks ('every birth is a miracle!'), urging me to focus on breathing, I understand addiction enough to forgive you and I am grateful that you were there for the end.

In retrospect, I feel sorry I was so intolerant towards your mother. But Pete, try to understand... The whole Lloyd clan and my mother were outside the door of the birthing suite. When your Mum arrived and you went out to see her and then popped your head in thirty seconds later and asked, 'Can Mum watch the birth, babe?', I couldn't think of anything more excruciating. When Braydon was born, it was just Richard and me... it was so intimate. With all those people waiting outside, Michael's birth felt like a spectator sport. I was in agony, bodily fluids everywhere and I was already naked by then. Try to understand, Pete, I didn't want anyone to see me like that except you (and, maybe, I was a little hurt that you couldn't sense that). Anyway,

I'm sorry I was less delicate in replying to your question than I should have been. I shouldn't have screamed 'Fuck off!' quite so loudly.

Call it a confession because I imagine it will give you some satisfaction... I have never told anyone this, but on these pages I will never send, I guess it's safe to share...

The night Michael was born, when it was nearly midnight, and you had left along with the entourage, I was cowering in the bathroom when the maternity ward nurse finally found me. I was hiding. Yes, hiding! She had to knock for a long time, before I was able to speak,

'I'll be out in a minute,' I said, my voice hoarse from crying.

'Please! The baby needs to be fed!'

You see, the first thing I noticed about my new-born son (besides the testicles, but that's a cliché!) was that he had your eyes. Those eyes that I had wished for made me flinch, can you imagine it, Pete? Naked, bleeding, exhausted, towering over my eight pound seven ounce son, I saw your eyes and, with a reflex that was still disturbingly new, I flinched.

I busied myself dressing, hoping no one had noticed. When talk of names came up, I mumbled agreement, still reeling from the feel of that flinch. And, seeing as I'm making confessions tonight, here's another one: I've always hated the name Michael.

But who was I to name this child, who made me shudder with his eyes? He looked so much like you when he was born, didn't he, Pete? Sometimes, in a stubborn expression, verging on a tantrum, I still see you in him and the resemblance feels so heavy to bear. But that shouldn't surprise you, Pete. I imagine that's why you don't bother to see him or call him, anymore. He is older and his face has changed. He has my eyes now.

V

*

She hated pot. It was funny. She was pretty open 'bout how much she missed shootin' up smack. Plus, I knew she'd banged up coke 'n' speed in the past. So she wasn't precious about drugs. She just didn't see the point of smokin' cones.

'I don't get it. People just sit around smoking not doing anything.'

'Unlike heroin, which is such a fucking motivating drug,' I shot back at 'er. She smiled,

'Touche,' she said and reached into 'er wallet for a tenner. I was hanging bad and tried to feel grateful. I really needed her to lend me twenty dollars.

I tried tellun 'er she might think different if she hung out with us, tried smokin' and stuff. She wasn't into the idea.

'I'm pregnant, for a start, Pete. Plus, it just isn't my thing.' Like I said, Steve, she could be a stuck-up snob when it came to drugs.

You know, mate, I woulda loved her no matter what. If she was by me side, while I was mullin' up or smokin' cones, that woulda been enough for me. But our life together wasn't enough for the stuck-up bitch.

She couldn't just be on the dole or the pension like the rest of us. *Noo*, she hadda go to uni 'n' get 'er degree. In March, she started goin' to uni twice a week. Suddenly, I was left to me own devices durin' the day. She was gone on the bus to take Braydon to day-care and go to 'er uni lectures in the mornin's by the time I got up.

What was that stupid subject she was studyun- Women's Studies? And didn't I hear 'bout it?! Women were- what was that word? -

oppressed. Yeah, poor her! She was gettin' a parentin' pension, gettin' cheap day-care 'n' bus trips. Yeah, she was bloody fuckin' oppressed!

She looked tired all the time. I called 'er on it.

'What are you tryin' to prove? You look tired all the time from studyin'... we never spend any time together anymore, and, whatcha think you're gunna get out of it? I don't see many job ads for lesbian feminists in the newspapers!' She didn't get precious, she just laughed. That blew me away a bit. I thought she was gunna get all posh 'n' precious.

'Pete, I don't want to live in these flats, forever.' Neither did I. I hated that the stuck-up bitch thought she was smart enough to get us outta there, but I didn't press the point. She'd grown up in the city. I'd been in this town almost all me life. I knew the truth. She couldn't see it, yet, but she'd soon see for 'erself. No one got outta places like this.

*

I tried takin' an interest, mate. I'm not a total prick. After she'd passed out one night, exhausted, after spendin' all night at the uni computers typin' up an essay to hand in the next day, I decided to have a squiz at what she was up to.

She was passed out on the dinin' room table. It was two in the mornin'. She'd gotten a lift home with one of her girlfriends from uni, who was crammin', too.

I tried to read the essay she was handin' in the next day. She had gone on and on about the fact it was the last one she needed to hand in so she could pass the unit. I was pretty sick 'bout hearin' 'bout it, frankly.

I was skullin' scotch that night; bein' pay day 'n' all, but I don't think it woulda made sense to me if I wasn't drinkin' either. Mumbo jumbo, all these big, lord it over ya words.

I'm not proud of what I did, Steve, but I just couldn't resist. It seemed like a bloody hilarious idea, at the time. You know, how sometimes when you're pissed, the stupidest things seem so funny? Well, mate, I was pretty pissed. I pulled out my cock and peed over the cover sheet. I watched me piss seepin' through, while I finished my bottla scotch, then I chucked the fancy essay in the toilet bowl 'n' staggered into bed 'n' passed out.

I woke up to 'er screamin'. She was hysterical, mate. I told 'er it was an accident.

'I'm sorry, babe, but you were so tired last night, ya know, maybe, you dropped it in the toilet while ya were readin' it in there. You were pretty fuckin' tired last night.' She was bawlin' her eyes out. I tried to cuddle 'er, but she pulled away. Slowly, she calmed down, breathed deep; her big belly movin' up 'n' down as she did. She worked out what she was gunna do. She jumped in the shower, got dressed, chucked the soakin' wet essay in a bag. She even remembered to kiss me quickly on the mouth, before she left.

'I'll catch the bus straight to uni. I've got to re-type this and hand it in before I pick up Braydon this afternoon. I don't know when I'll be home.'

*

She was supposed to be at uni returning some library books, when she rang me at Mum's. She sounded puffed on the phone.

'I'm going into labour. I'm on my way to the hospital.' I was working on Mum at the time for some cash so I could score a stick. Mum was at least an hour away from sayun 'yes'. I knew I had a bitta time up my sleeve, before she was in full on labour or anythin'.

'I'll meet you at the hospital later.' It worked out well. I was 'bout to be a father. I was gunna be stuck at hospital. Mum found some cash

92

for me to catch a taxi to the hospital. I spent it on pot. We mulled up, smoked some cones 'n' then I got a ride into the hospital with you, Steve, remember?

She decided she was gunna do it all as naturally as possible. She'd had the works with 'er first kid and she felt like it'd 'dulled' (her word, not mine!) the experience. She was just gunna use gas this time …

'You've just gotta push now, dear,' the mid-wife said. She pushed, groaning 'er lungs out. All she could manage was a turd. I couldn't help meself. I started pissin' meself laughin'. She started cryin'; she was frustrated and angry at 'erself. I tried to reach for 'er and she just waved me away and locked 'erself in the bath-room 'n' started bawlin'. The whole scene was pretty intense.

The stuck-up mid-wife pulled me aside to gimme a lecture.

'You've gotta support her better. I know it seems like it's taking ages, but think about what it's like for her.' I nodded. The stupid mid-wife had no idea. This labour thing had been goin' on for hours! My whole family was outside waitin' for this kid to be born and I was hangin' out. I just wanted it over and done with so I could go 'n' score.

Me mother was outside because *she* didn't want anyone, but me, in the delivery room. Well, what about *me*? I coulda used Mum in there. Like I said, it was pretty fucking intense! I had stuff I was dealin' with, too. The mid-wife had no idea!

I smiled at the dopey mid-wife and told 'er,

'Look, I'm sorry… It's me first time.' She laughed.

'Okay, let's do it!' the mid-wife said, like a football coach trying to psych up 'er team.

93

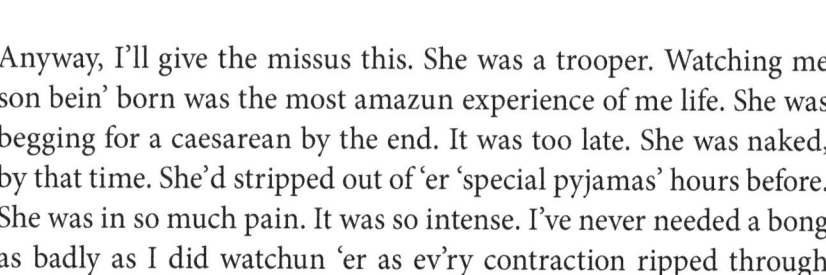

Anyway, I'll give the missus this. She was a trooper. Watching me son bein' born was the most amazun experience of me life. She was begging for a caesarean by the end. It was too late. She was naked, by that time. She'd stripped out of 'er 'special pyjamas' hours before. She was in so much pain. It was so intense. I've never needed a bong as badly as I did watchun 'er as ev'ry contraction ripped through 'er. When no one was lookun, I swiped some of 'er gas. I don't think I woulda survived otherwise.

He was born and it was beautiful. I forgot about wantin' to score just like that! I was a father.

I still remember what she said. I was lookun at my son, *my son,* mullin' over those two amazin' words. All she saw were his big, bloated balls and she said, real softly, 'er voice tired and defeated,

'It's a boy! Poor Braydon!' She thought, until the day she died, I didn't hear 'er, but I did. I knew exactly what she meant. We thought me son was gunna be a girl. I wanted to call our daughter Catherine, after Mum, and she had 'er heart set on some feral name, like Phoenix, or somethin'. Ultrasound technology wasn't what it is today, you know.

Anyway, maybe, she was right. It woulda been easier if he had been a girl. And look, I know she was out of it on gas, but I will never forgive 'er for ruinin' the most mind-blowing moment of me life.

She wouldn't hold him. She was standun there, naked, the umbilical cord still uncut, lookin' at this screaming baby with balls. I was rapt. This was *my* son. She was paralysed. Even the mid-wife thought the whole scene was strange.

'Who wants to hold him?' the mid-wife asked, a little uncomfortably.

'You do it,' she said.

'Are you sure?' She nodded tiredly. He wasn't a girl. She didn't give a damn. I held him and they cut the umbilical cord. She got busy, dressun.

Her mother came up with the idea of callin' him Michael, after Mum's Dad, Mick. Mum was stoked, but *she* didn't seem to give a damn. She had no interest in the conversation about what to call our son. He wasn't a girl. She hated 'er father so she sure as hell wasn't gunna name our baby after him.

'Yeah, whatever,' she said. She looked exhausted and like she couldn't care less. Everyone in me family was in love with this little boy. They'd all come to the hospital to support 'er. She was such a skank that only 'er Mum was there- everyone else in *her* family hated 'er and wouldn't speak to 'er anymore. When she said, 'Whatever' I was furious. This was me son. This was me mother's first grandson. This was me Grandad's namesake. Was she really that fucking thick?

Oh, I smiled for the camera. She did too. But I hated 'er. As I looked into the camera, holding me son and smilin', I thought, angrily, 'You can't get away with ruinin' me son's birth. Ruin anythun, but not me son's birth.'

To be fair to 'er, mate, I think, at the time, I was a bit hard on 'er. Look, she ruined the moment. It's unforgivable, but, like I said, I've had lotsa time in here to think about stuff. I think she saw our baby's balls and froze. Suddenly, she had two boys. She knew I was gunna treat this one differently. If Michael had been a girl, there mighta been a chance I'd bond with Braydon over boy stuff. Now there was no hope and she knew it.

The chick was smart and manic. In the first thirty seconds of me son's life, exhausted from giving birth, she still couldn't switch 'er brain off. She was doin' the calculations in 'er head, thinking ahead to how it was gunna be and the image in 'er head of the years she had ahead of 'er was depressun as hell.

Like I said, I hate 'er for ruinin' the moment. There's no excuse for what she did, but I can almost understand why she did it.

She joked that she'd be sucking me off lots. I wasn't supposed to 'ave sex with 'er for six weeks. She was true to her word. The blow jobs were fast 'n' furious.

It didn't work for me…I made it three days, after she got outta the hospital. She hadn't put on much weight during the pregnancy and 'er figure bounced back pretty quick. You couldn't tell she'd 'ad a kid about a week after she gave birth. Except, 'er tits were huge. If, anything, that made 'er sexier. I didn't care how bloody she was. She was still warm. She was still wet.

She looked at me bloody, red cock, as I pulled outta 'er and 'er face fell. I didn't care. I think 'er shame turned me on even more. I dunno, mate. I only know I wanted 'er more than ever after she'd had our kid.

The little dweeb, Braydon, was at 'is grandmother's and we were at Mum's with the new baby. We were in the guest room; next door to Mum's room. That made the sex even more excitun. We hadda be quiet, 'coz Mum was in the next room and I'll tell you what, mate, it wasn't easy for 'er. She was a moaner and a screamer.

It was like a holiday, with this little baby in the corner interrupting, ev'ry couple of hours, during the night. It didn't matter, to me. It was my son, *my* little man. I loved that she'd given me this gift. Being a father was amazin'.

*

She hated bein' there. She wasn't a first-time mum and Mum tried to treat 'er like she was. I think she had hard feelin's about the fact that Mum assumed she couldn't bathe a baby or change a nappy. Mum was just tryin' to be helpful, ya know, Steve. She shoulda been grateful she wasn't all by 'erself washun the mountains of dirty baby clothes a new-born creates. Mum was just doin' her best to help, ya know. Mum didn't know much about 'er, just that she'd been on the 'done, that she'd lost custody of 'er other kid for close to a year, so she assumed she'd need to start from scratch. Mum didn't do it to piss 'er off, or anythin', but the selfish cow resented Mum's interferun.

She couldn't shit and she had haemorrhoids. Michael would never feed properly, so she was pullun out 'er tits nine or ten times a day to feed 'im. I'll give 'er this. It couldna been fun for 'er, but, Steve, she was a mother now. She shoulda just sucked it up and gotten on with it.

'You got a new baby,' I said. 'You should be grateful Mum wants to help ya out!'

'We can't stay here forever. Braydon has to come home.'

She made it six days and then she put 'er foot down.

'I'm going home,' she said. It was ten at night and Mum was in bed. She'd just finished feedun Michael and puttin' 'im in the bassinet.

'Then fucking take him now!' I said. 'He's not mine anyway, you fucking slut! He's prob'ly Gazza's or some other guy's. Do you even know, you fucking slag?' Oh, you can be sure, she did that whole 'victim' thing again. First there were tears, then the bawlin' and then she looked at me; 'er eyes were beggin'.

'Please, Pete' she whispered. 'Don't do this.' I pushed at 'er in bed 'til she fell over the edge. I heard 'er body slam onto the floor.

'Take him home now, you fucking slut.' It killed me to say it. This was me son, but I was damned if she was gunna hold that over me.

I think she slept in the livin' room on the sofa. She was there in the mornin', breast-feeding our son in 'er pyjamas. Mum was sittun there drinkin' a cuppa and they were laughin' politely about somethin'. She didn't say a word. She looked up at me. Her mouth was set. Her eyes seemed to say, 'Are you going to tell her or am I going to tell her what you did to me last night?'

I knew it was decision time. I knew Mum wanted us to stay.

But she couldn't handle it. She wanted to go home and get 'er little prick to come home from his grandmother's. For once, in 'er fucking life, the liberated feminist put the decision back on me.

'We're goin' 'ome today, Mum.' Mum was devastated. Her face fell. It killed me to do it to 'er. It was one more thing I couldn't forgive that crazy bitch for.

'Look, we'll still be over all the time. This is a much more hygienic environment for him to have baths and such,' she said. Mum knew she was pissin' in 'er pocket. I decided, there and then, to make sure it happened. I didn't care I had no car and that it was a thirty minute walk. Me mother was gunna see her grandson ev'ry day.

Mum drove us home. Steve, I'll never forget it, Mum's face was ash grey, as she pulled into the car-park of those crappy flats. This was the dive where her baby grandson was living. Can you blame Mum?

She didn't give a shit. She'd gotten 'er way. She was all smug and 'er son got dropped off that night. But I wasn't lettun 'er get away with it. I'd bide me time, Steve, but she wasn't fucking gettin' away with it!

I was back there, when I coulda been at home with Mum. Mum and I were connecting for the first time in years, for fuck's sake! Didn't she get how important that was to me? How could she take that away from me? I couldn't let 'er get away with it. She'd broken Mum's heart. She'd ruined me first moment with me son. The bitch hadda pay.

Letter 8

Local News, 28 July 2001

Slavic Ramchen, a millionaire business-man was granted bail by a Supreme Court judge yesterday, after being charged with the murder of his wife in Melbourne. His wife disappeared nine years ago, after dropping the children off at school. Police had been called to their residence two weeks before the disappearance. Mrs Ramchen had rung police to report an incident of domestic violence, resulting in her hair being pulled out and some facial bruising.

Dear Pete,

*A*re there places that resonate for you, Pete? For a long time, the Federal Court Building, in the city, has resonated with a roar that hits me hard in the pit of my stomach. Years ago, I used to walk past it, trekking from the city to university and I was indifferent to it. It never spoke to me.

Now, when I walk through the sliding glass doors of that building to go into Family Court, I need to take a deep breath every time. I remind myself I am there to do a job, but every time I cross that thresh-hold, my body feels the memories of being found wanting. These days I am always dressed in a very expensive suit, but my heart still skips a beat. Years ago, it was here that I felt the most exposed- first with Richard and then with you. Sometimes, I finger the lapels of my jacket- as if to make sure that I really am not naked.

Over a year before we commenced our own hostilities in those dark, wood-panelled court rooms, your instincts for eroding my sense of self were already acute and, with the honed impulses of a predator, you knew just how to annihilate me. Do you remember, Pete? Gone were the days, when you toyed with words like 'slut' and 'posh' to verbally assault me. Packing Michael's baby things into that huge pram (more suburban utility vehicle than sleek stroller), whilst detailing how you would destroy me in Family Court was much more efficient. Missile precise, the memory of those taunts, still makes me shudder.

'Even a court's said what a shit-house mother you are, for fuck's sake! That's why you weren't allowed to have ya kid with you all that time!' you would say.

I can by no means recall every incident, but I can still remember the rhythm of our days. Sleepless, tired from persisting with those bus trips to deliver Braydon to his beloved child-care centre (by then, my insistence on continuity of care for my son, was an almost pathological compulsion), I would inadvertently offend you.

Then, all bets were off weren't they, Pete? You would clench your teeth, call me a 'slut' or a 'cunt' and then you would start throwing Michael's things loudly into a bag, telling me in excruciating detail about how you were going to screw me in Family Court.

A few times, when I tried to stop you, you pushed me out of the way. That's how that photo of me, as a laughing, nineteen-year-old uni student, lost its place on the mantlepiece and became relegated to the pages of a photo album.

Sometimes, I have to confess, the offence was passively-aggressively deliberate. A father now, you had taken to staking your territory in that flat by sitting buddha-like on that hideous blue, velvet bean bag (it was the only item of furniture you had brought with you when you first moved in with me) and loudly slurping up cones of marijuana, while I went about my business. On these pages you will never read, I can finally admit that it pissed the hell out of me.

Accustomed to your mother's manic ministrations, you seemed oblivious to the fact that we were not living in the fifties anymore. You refused to change a nappy. You never did the dishes or threw a load of clothes into the washing machine. Did you even realise what a clothes line was for, Pete? You scanned the job ads with a kind of perfunctoriness and humoured me, by calling out, whilst I was trimming the crusts off sandwiches for Braydon's lunch,

'What about this one? They wanna labourer at that new estate. I could prob'ly organise lifts to work with Andy... what d'ya reckon, babe?'

The charade became teeth-grittingly excruciating, after a while. It was difficult to fake the requisite enthusiasm you expected. When the rent was due or the electricity bill arrived, you were always conveniently absent. At first, the excuses were imaginative. Later, we both stopped bothering with the pretence. I stopped expecting a financial contribution and you stopped pretending to look for jobs. I became resigned to the fact that smoking bongs was the only career you could commit to.

At that time, my resentment had not yet had time to marinate and I tolerated our surreal, sleepless, mysoginistic universe with a merciful, good humour that is hard to stir up, now. (Pete, at times, I even believed that there was something wrong with me!) Folding laundry, while listening to Lifehouse's 'Hanging by A Moment', one night, when the boys were down for the night and you were out (of course, you were out, the rent was due!), I reached with desperation for a diagnosis. Perhaps, this was post-natal depression.

The women's health nurse was exceedingly kind. She listened to my story with compassionate eyes. She said with sympathetic softness in her tone,

'I just think you've been through a lot of things that make it okay to feel sad.' Even in my sleep-deprived zombie state, her meaning did not elude me. ('You're not depressed because you've just had a baby. You're depressed because your life sucks!')

Sometimes, there were jangling, off-key notes in the bleak rhythm of our life. I was, somehow, obliviously, tone-deaf to them. Michael's christening is a matter of public record of course, like too many other incidents in our life together, but there were many episodes that winter that I have dutifully kept secret.

Do you remember the first time you pinned me against the wall, 'Butt out bitch,' you said, with your forearm against my neck. I was still gasping for air, when you grabbed Michael and stormed out the door.

As always, I didn't know if you were coming back. Every time you left with Michael, you implied that you were leaving for good. When you would return, you would always mutter, 'He needs a feed' or 'He needs a change.' My relief was pathetic. I was always disgusted with myself, but I had learnt, by then, that it was wiser to keep my mouth shut. So, I would make pitiful chatter about what you wanted for dinner, gushing in my unspoken gratitude. You had brought my son back! Yay! Thinking back on it now, I feel sick. Our conspiracy of silence was obscene.

Remembering those first few months of Michael's life, as I write this, I feel a burning, red-faced sense of humiliation. I have eviscerated Armani-clad solicitors in court-rooms with my biting wit. I have challenged magistrates by citing obscure case law in a steady, assertive voice. I am mortified to think that I once danced to such different tunes. Even today, standing at the bar table, I have to take a deep, slow breath before I start oral submissions. When I exhale, I let go of that quivering, jittery mouse of a woman that once inspired our mutual scorn.

V

*

I'm not proud of some of the shit I did. But I was so fucking angry! I had the right to be. This was me son. She wasn't gunna fuck him up like she'd fucked up 'er faggotty kid.

*

From the start, she did a half-assed job of mothering Michael. Steve, I'm the first to admit it. I'm not perfect. I promised 'er I was gunna give up the dope the night me son was born. And yes, I was suckin' down cones like there was no tomorrow, with you, the next day... but, for fuck's sake!

The house was always a fuckin' mess. She cared more 'bout catchin' those fuckin' buses to get Braydon to day-care than cleanin' up. She was always tired so sometimes she was hard to wake up in the middle o' the night. Poor little Michael sometimes screamed for ages before she woke up 'n' got busy feedun 'im.

Remember Andy's Maddie? How wild was she when she first started going out with Andy?!

Then, after she gave birth to their daughter, she was all about bein' a mother, remember? Yeah, Maddie was a fat nag sometimes, but she knew 'ow to be a mother; and this was a chick, who was pregnant at seventeen! She breast-fed their little girl, Maddie Junior, until she was two. She didn't drink, she didn't smoke and she was nice to Andy. Their flat was always spotless. Maddie went over to Mum's with Maddie Junior ev'ry day, while Andy was at work. They planned her dream weddin' together. Mum even made Maddie's weddin' dress! Mum loved Maddie. But Mum never quite connected with the mother of my child. I don't blame Mum.

Like I said, Mum loved Maddie to bits, but me missus didn't think much of Maddie.

'I'm not spending every day at your mother's shooting the breeze, like Maddie. I have things to do and I don't need to be supervised, when I give my son a bath,' she told me in a pissy voice, when we were back home. Like I said, I hate it when stuck-up bitches try to lay down the law, ya know, so I put me foot down from the start.

'They're not brothers,' I said and I meant it. That ferret-faced prick was nothing to me son.

She paid lip service to me orders. She pretended to agree, but she was a sneaky, little bitch. She went to playgroups with 'er 'two sons'. She caught two buses to take Braydon to day-care and took me son with 'er. She'd read stories to them both on the bus and taught 'er son to play peek-a-boo with me Michael.

I hadda fix it. I'm not a prick. I didn't like doin' it, but I had to.

She didn't see it comin'; thought it was a normal Saturdee. I hated that she had *her* son with 'er. It was supposed to be 'er weekend off from the little prick. It took me a while to work meself up to do what I needed to do, but, when I had it mapped out in me head, and Michael was asleep after a feed, I faced her, looked 'er in the eye, tried not to sound too pissed off.

'Does he understand what I am to you?' She was so fucking stupid. She just stared at me like a fucking retard. I called Braydon in from his room. 'Sit there, Braydon,' I said pointing to the sofa. I sat on the arm chair and pulled down me fly. I looked at her. I was staunch, when I said it, 'Suck me off.'

'He's just there…' she said, shyly. She didn't think I'd go through with it. I just looked 'er in the eye. I didn't cringe. It was make or

106

break time. She looked in me eyes and she saw ev'ry little thing I had to hold over her- Gazza, the receivin' stolen goods charge, ev'ry dirty little heroin addict secret she'd been stupid nuff to tell me.

She knew I'd do it, too. She knew I'd get on the phone to the kid's grandmother. I'd sign an affidavit, if the old hag wanted me to. I'd get meself a suit to wear to court 'n' testify, if Braydon's grandmother needed me to. She'd lose custody of Braydon in a heart-beat. I didn't have to say a word. Sometimes, it was like that with us, Steve. We didn't need to talk. It was one of those moments. She saw it in me eyes.

'Now!' I said.

She did it; on her knees, with her son watchin', usin' her hands to try 'n' hide what she was doin' from 'im. I wasn't a total prick. I let 'er get away with *that*.

When she was finished, cum drippun down 'er chin, her eyes looked dead. I pulled her head up by the back of 'er hair so she was lookin' me in the eye.

'They're not brothers, okay? Get it?' She got my meaning. She nodded. She looked broken and sad 'n' she had that whole 'victim' thing happenin' again.

I hated that I hadda do it, Steve, but it was the only way to make the bitch understand! If you didn't rub her nose in it, she'd walk around goin', 'Yes, yes' in that sweet, piss in ya pocket voice, then doin' whatever the fuck she wanted and actun as if she didn't have a clue.

She started leavin' me son with me when she caught the bus to take Braydon to day-care. It was a pain in the ass, sometimes, when Michael was cranky, but it was worth it. She'd express milk before she left and she wasn't gone that long that I couldn't wait for her to get back to change 'is nappy if he was wet or dirty, so it was all good and, at the end of the day, I'd made me point. They weren't fucking brothers. End of fucking story.

*

When we christened Michael, I put me foot down again.

'Braydon stays with his Gran that day. He's not welcome. This is *my* son's day.'

She resented it. I know that. All day, she and her mother were whisperin' in their language in corners. Her Mum was lovely. I never had a problem with her Mum and I always had a heapa time for her Mum, but when they spoke to each other- in Cuban, I think it was- you always felt like they were talkun 'bout ya.

I wasn't gunna let 'er ruin the day, though. I had a coupla beers with you 'n' Andy. Me mate came in from outta town and he gushed over the baby. Tina, the godmother, was stoked. It was a good day all round. I didn't let her broodin' in the corner bother me.

We were back at her flat by nine o'clock. Me mother had gone to all that work… and Mum was alone by nine o'clock. I was furious with the broodin', mopey cunt for doin' that to me Mother.

I grabbed the back of 'er neck and put the phone up to 'er ear, after I'd dialled Mum's number.

'Ask her if she's okay, you bitch!' She did it.

'Your Mum's fine,' she said. Her voice was cold and hard. She had this funny look in 'er eye. I didn't trust it, so I put me hands 'round 'er neck and squeezed,

'You got somethin' to say?' I squeezed until 'er eyes closed and then let go. She collapsed to the floor. Fucking ballsy bitch- she woulda let me kill her!

She'd dialled the police station as soon as she'd gotten off the phone to Mum. She'd left the phone off the hook,

'You choked me,' she said real loud, when she came to.

'Shut up, you psycho bitch,' I said. I didn't know the police were listenin', but I saw the phone was off the hook and I hung it up.

The police showed up not long after and took me down to the station. I rang Mum to come 'n' pick me up and I made Mum drop me back at her place. Mum tried to convince me it was a bad idea.

'Pete,' Mum was urgin' me, 'Just come to my house for the night.'

'No, Mum, it'll be fine. I know exactly how to play this. We're not leavin' your grandson alone with that psycho bitch, so drop me off there.' I knew that would convince Mum. She dropped me off just like I wanted.

'Fucking scared, are you? Then why did you let me back in, you fucking slut?' I pushed the door open, missin' 'er face by inches and I walked towards 'er, me teeth clenched, me fists ready... I was so mad at her! They'd finger-printed me, locked me up, while they took their time about writin' out me bail conditions.

She didn't flinch. Her eyes were cold. She pointed at 'er neck. I could see the marks where I'd pressed me thumbs into 'er throat.

'Look at what you did to me and tell me that's okay.' That's all she said. She went to bed; left me standun there. She wasn't scared. She was staunch 'n' ballsy. She'd said what she hadda say and left the room. Sometimes, it was like that with us. She could say a word or a sentence in this cool, calm voice and reduce you to nothin'.

I slipped into bed, lay lookin' at her. She wasn't asleep. She flinched when I lifted my hand. I stroked 'er cheek softly.

'I'm sorry,' I said, rubbing me thumb over 'er lips real soft. I focused on keepin' me voice real gentle.

'Well, it's not okay,' she said. She was tryin' to sound hard-ass, but she was comin' 'round, I could tell.

'You know this day meant so much to Mum…' I was still focused on soundin' real gentle, forced meself to forget the scene at the police station. Otherwise, I wasn't gunna be able to pull it off.

'Yes, I know. It meant a lot to me, too, Pete.' I stroked her throat, massagin' it with me thumbs, felt 'er shiver, for a second. I massaged the bruises real softly, lettin' her feel 'ow sorry I was supposed to be.

'I just didn't want 'er to be alone. But you gotta know how sorry I am, babe.' She nodded. I kept the rage outta my voice, when I spoke again, said it like I was tellin' 'er she needed to make a cuppa tea, real casual. I'll tell you what, Steve, it wasn't fucking easy! 'You gotta ring the police tomorrow and drop the charges, you know that. You don't want 'em to put me in jail, do ya?'

'No, of course not,' she whispered.

'Then you'll do it, won't ya?' She nodded and I pulled 'er gently into me arms and kissed the top of her head, 'Thank you, babe. I really *am* sorry.'

'I know,' she said, before we fell asleep.

The sex the next mornin' was incredible. I fucked 'er real hard for a very long time. She was beggin' for me to come, tellin' me I was hurting 'er, when I stopped short, 'You'll do it today, won't you bitch?' I didn't start moving me cock inside 'er again until I heard the word, 'yes.' She said it in a small, husky voice and I started thrustin', again… hard and fast 'till I came.

*

Steve, I know I sound like a total prick, but it's so hard to explain how she drove me to this place. She fucked with me head- *ev'ry* minute of *ev'ry* day. It was in what she wore and 'ow she spoke.

She believed her sons were brothers and, even after I'd made her suck me off in front of Braydon, she'd find all these little ways to undermine me. The playgroups went on behind me back while I was hung-over and asleep. She'd be back, just as I was wakin' up. She just didn't get it.

All these things she did... just to push me buttons. I wished I'd been stronger, but it got to me 'coz I loved 'er. I'd be fuckin' furious with her over somethun, clenchin' me teeth, ballin' me fists, ready to smash that fucking beautiful face and me cock would be gettin' hard, if ya can fucking believe it! Just *lookin'* at 'er could reduce me just like that!

I hated that she had that power over me. I hated it, man!

*

She hardly ever said no, but this one mornin' she did. 'I don't feel like it. Michael's been up all night and I'm tired.' I slipped me cock between 'er clenched butt cheeks 'n' just shoved it into 'er.

'You know you want it!' I said. I could feel 'er drippin' on me cock. 'See! You're wet!' I whispered into her ear.

I dunno what it was about that mornin', but she wasn't havin' it. She tensed 'er back. She tried to pull away, but I held her in place with both me hands, digging me finger-nails into her hips and I kept fucking her.

Her voice was hard, firm and so fucking posh, as she stopped wrigglin',

'Let me explain this in terms you can understand, Pete. You need to get your cock out of my cunt *now* before I have you charged with *rape*.'

I pulled out quick smart. I knew she meant business and there was nothin' I could do to stop 'er. The bitch knew what cards to play, all right!

I let it go that day, but a coupla days later, when we were sittun outside, drinkin' ginger beer, I told 'er,

'I reckon if you raped someone these days you'd have to kill 'em. It's too easy to get caught, these days.' I looked 'er straight in the eye. It wasn't a threat; just a statement of fact. To be honest, I didn't really know where I was goin' with it, yet.

'It's a difficult crime to convict, though. It's his word against hers.' She'd studied the law so she knew what she was goin' on about. She was so fucking smart and I know she must've seen me relax a bit. From that, she knew exactly what I was gettin' at and, for some reason, it was important to her to make the point. She looked me in the eye, took a swig of 'er ginger beer, 'Mind you, who wants the headfuck?' She smiled at me then. It was a fucking smug smile.

*

At the end of the day, though, I knew she was not as smart as she thought she was. She got so screwed in the custody battle over 'er eldest son. Considering she'd done law, that was a pretty sad state of affairs. The judge musta thought she was an incredible skank to make 'er share 'er son with her ex. I never let 'er forget it.

'You're an ex-junkie, no judge in 'is right mind is ever gunna forget that, you know. Ya know what they say, don't ya? Once a junkie, always a junkie. I reckon if I took you to court, I'd get custody.' Her lip shivered.

'You probably would.'

*

She frustrated me so much sometimes, Steve. I never told you how the Department of Children's Services (DoCS) got involved with us. Part of it was the police chargin' me with assault the night Michael was christened (in the end, she couldn't withdraw the charges because the police had charged me *not* her), but a lot of other times the police got called because I'd man-handle 'er a bit, shove 'er away, grab Michael and take off to Mum's. I wasn't gunna let 'er forget this was me son and when she did somethin' that pissed me off, I reminded 'er who was boss.

'I'm leaving you bitch and I'm takin' me son! He's gunna live with me and me Mum, you crazy cunt!'

She'd try 'n' stop me and I'd get physical. Then she'd ring the police. Stupid bitch! She'd just been so devastated by losin' Braydon to her ex and his Gran for a year that she couldn't help 'erself. The cops'd turn up and ask what was goin' on and she wouldn't be able to bring 'erself to say anythin'. She knew if DoCS got involved, she'd be totally fucked. She'd probably lose both kids and that woulda killed 'er, Steve. I knew it and she knew it.

And she knew, just days after I choked 'er that DoCS *would* get involved. When the DoCS guy came to the door, I hid in the next room.

Apparently, the police had notified DoCS when they came to charge me with assault. Apparently, the cops did that ev'ry time they got called and there were kids around.

'So what happened?' the DoCS guy asked. Like I said, the bitch was fuckin' manic 'n' smart. She took a breath 'n' she knew just how to play it. Her voice was posh and she sounded so incredibly convincing in her 'lord it over you' voice. I was so proud of 'er.

'Look, it's over. I told him to leave. It's simple. He tried to choke me. I've done a university major in Women's Studies. I know that isn't acceptable. He hasn't been back since.' She was fucking smooth. I bit me tongue to stop from laughing in the next room. He bought 'er story. She was a fucking good liar. He left us alone.

But, after that, she knew how easy it'd be to lose the kids. She could bring 'erself to ring the cops when I man-handled 'er so I could take off with Michael, but she couldn't bring 'erself to follow through. Like I said, Steve, she could talk the talk, but she couldn't walk the walk. It was handy to know. There was no way she could ever go through with somethin' that'd land the father of her child in jail.

One time, I pushed her onto the livin' room floor and told 'er I was takin' Michael. I started packin' me things. I hadn't left yet when the cops arrived. I heard her talkun to the cop. Her voice was tired 'n' empty, Steve.

'There's nothing you can do. I'm sorry I rang. It won't happen again.'

*

Like I said, the kids ruined us, as a couple, Steve. She was forever fucking tired. She'd get lippy because of lacka sleep, when she shoulda known better.

Steve, she never believed me, but I swear it's true. I never set out to start hitting 'er. She reckoned with all 'er feminist bull-shit that I was just workin' me way up to it with the comments about 'er clothes in the early days. She had pamphlets about domestic violence that she'd leave lyin' 'round, after I'd tried chokin' 'er. She'd start recitin' them when we were fighting.

'It's not okay for you to undermine me all the time,' she'd say in her posh, superior voice.

'Yeah, well, it's not okay for you to be such a stuck-up, psycho bitch.'

I was so fucking frustrated, that day. I was hanging out. I was broke. It was our brother, Andy's buck's night and she was holdin' out on me. I knew she 'ad cash, Steve.

We were in the community housing flat by then. Nicer class of neighbours. She was outside, in the courtyard, tryin' to get away from me. She kept tellin' me to leave 'er alone. She didn't want 'er precious son to see us fighting. That's why she'd gone outside.

'I'm not giving you any cash, Pete. I need what I have for nappies. I am not going down to the Salvation Army begging for nappies *again* this week just so you can smoke weed and drink all the time. I'm tired of it. You never give me a financial contribution for anything. I can't pay the bills with your semen.' I slapped the lippy bitch then. Her face was outraged. She wasn't gunna take that lightly.

'I'm sorry,' I said, pressin' me hands down onto 'er shoulders so I could calm 'er down. She pulled away, I kept me voice soft, to calm 'er down. 'Come inside now. We'll talk it over.' I grabbed 'er by the arm. She pulled away and fell.

'No!' She was lyin' down on the ground now.

'See what you've done,' I said, 'You're comin' inside now.'

'No, I'm not.' I grabbed 'er by the hair and started draggun her into the flat.

'You are fucking coming inside now. You can do it standin' up or lyin' down. It's up to you.' She started screamun. She sounded fucking crazy, so I stopped, let go of 'er hair, slapped 'er face over and over a few times- just to calm 'er down. I realised the neighbours might be watchin' and yelled at the top of me lungs, 'You stupid drunk bitch!'

She was in tears, when she gave me the money. She was cryin' in that defeated, right down to the bones tone women get sometimes, you know? I used some of the cash she'd given me to slip into the stripper's g-string that night and thought of 'er devastated face. I tried not to let it get me down. It was me brother's night. I wasn't gunna let 'er ruin it.

*

By that time, Mum was tellin' me to leave 'er. You were doin' the same thing, Steve, but … I just couldn't let go.

Remember that Saturdee afternoon, we were out for beers and bets, and you tried to convince me to leave 'er? I worked it out, mate. Mum asked you to have a man-to-man with me.

'She's a promiscuous bitch,' you said. Big fucking word for you, Steve! I knew you meant business. 'You know what she did with Gazza.' You looked at me hard. 'Just get the kid and leave. You know Mum'll back you up. We all will.' I drank me first beer slowly and sadly.

'I can't. I love her, man.'

'Pete, can you stop thinkin' with your dick, mate? You know where this is fucking headin'! She's not gonna rest until you're in jail.'

'It's not *all* her fault,' I said, defendin' her. 'She's got a lot goin' on. I'm a pain sometimes, when I don't have enough dope.'

'She's a junkie, mate. Maybe, she's off the spoon, right now, but she's still a fucking junkie! She's crazy! She doesn't care whose life she screws up. She's been a junkie for too long and that's all she knows. Fucking people over is *all* she knows.' I finished me beer.

'Maybe you're right.'

Crazy Bitch inside_Updated.indd   116

3/31/2012   7

Maybe, you were, right mate, but I couldn't bring meself to end it 'n', besides, the truth was she may 'ave been a shit-house mother, but she kept the kids fed, she made sure Michael was dry 'n' clean, she got Braydon to day-care in clean clothes. She did all the things Mum did for us. I didn't know if I coulda handled all those little details involved in bein' a parent, all by meself. As weak as it sounds, I was scared to try.

One time I found 'er in the mornin' sittun on the sofa, crying. Michael was asleep in 'is bassinet, but it'd been a rough night. She was holdin' one of the photos we'd taken at the hospital. She looked so fuckin' tired, mate,

'Babe, what's wrong?' I asked 'er, real gentle. She looked up at me 'n' 'er face was so devastated.

'Maybe, you're right, Pete,' she said and she was cryin' so hard 'er whole body was shakin', 'I don't think I'm up to this. Maybe, it's better if you take him to live with your mother.' Her voice was breakun when she said it. It had killed her to say it out loud, mate. I could see it in 'er eyes. I'm not a total prick. So, I sat on the sofa next to her 'n' pulled 'er into me arms.

'C'mon, babe, stop cryin'. You're just tired, babe,' I whispered 'n' I kissed the top of her head and she bawled into me chest so she wouldn't wake Michael. I rocked her real gently, 'n' let 'er cry for a bit, then I said real soft, 'Ring Sarah and tell 'er to keep Braydon tonight, okay, babe. I'll take Michael to Mum's for a few hours. You just get yourself some sleep, okay?' She wiped 'er eyes with the back of 'er hand 'n' nodded, but she still looked so defeated.

After I got back from Mum's, I just sat on the edge o' the bed and watched her sleep and it was one of those times... It's hard to describe, Steve, but I just felt so lucky.

ch inside_Updated.indd 117 3/31/2012 7:24:26 PM

Later, after I picked Michael up, I put 'im down with a bottle of her expressed milk. She was just startin' to wake up. 'Shh,' I whispered. She watched me coverin' 'im up and slipped quietly over 'n' rubbed me back. We crept outta Michael's room and had noodles for dinner together, sittun at the table not really talkin' and, every now and then, I'd just reach over 'n' squeeze her hand. She looked less tired 'n' she was lookun beautiful again. It was nice.

*

Sometimes, it was fucking hard to remember why I was there, though! One night she pushed me buttons so hard, I packed me bags, packed Michael's things, walked Michael, in his pram, with all our stuff in it, up to Mum's. The cops rang me at Mum's from the hospital.

'She's out of control,' Mum said. Mum's mouth was really tight. 'You've gotta do something.'

I'd cracked 'er ribs shovin' her a few weeks before. She was demandin' ex-rays. She done a urine test, too. She was yellun at me as I came up the drive-way to the emergency ward.

'I've done a urine test, Pete! You can't claim I'm doing this because I'm a junkie, you bastard!' She was hysterical. A nurse was holdin' 'er back, as she went off 'er brain.

'Look mate, she's breast-feeding. She's worried about you taking off with the kid like that,' the female cop, said calmly. In an instant, I knew how to play it. 'She's had an ex-ray. The break's probably an old one so there's nothing we can really do about it. You need to let her take the baby home.' I knew the cop couldn't make me give 'er me kid. She couldn't even prove I'd cracked 'er ribs. That's why the cop was tryin' so hard to sound calm, reasonable and nice

'I dunno if I can do that,' I said. I was scared shitless, because I don't like talkun to cops, but I knew I hadda sound calm. 'She came off the methadone just before she got pregnant with our son, you know. She went a bit crazy after that. I just went up to visit my Mum with my son. I never tried to take him away. I dunno what she's goin' on about.' Me lies came out real smoothly. I faked bein' concerned, 'I'm worried about leavin' her alone with him.' I concentrated on keepin' me voice calm and reasonable; her madness was more likely to stand out, that way, I figured.

I watched as her face fell. She was on the other side of the emergency ward and the cops were talkun to 'er. I couldn't hear a word, but I could see 'er face. I watched as 'er body sagged and I knew I'd pulled it off.

They weren't gunna let 'er take him home without me. My son and I were *the package deal* now.

'Mum said I should start callin' DoCS on *you!*' I told her that night. Me voice was bold 'n' proud. Her voice was hard 'n' husky 'n' broken.

'I *know* this is happening to me. I *know* I'm not going crazy. You are a despicable piece of shit, who bashes women.' She wasn't angry. She said it like it was a matter of fact.

'Look, I've never bashed anyone in me life except you.' (That wasn't strictly true. I got charged with punchin' Mum that time, remember? But that wasn't the point!) 'Maybe you need to take a long hard look at yourself. Even the police wouldn't let you bring ya son home by yourself tonight.'

Letter 9

In Brief: The findings in the September 2001-released report, *Young Australians and Domestic Violence* are startling. The study of 5,000 Australians aged between 12 and 20 has found that up to one quarter of respondents have witnessed physical domestic against their mother or stepmother.

Dear Pete,

*J*ust as our parents' generation could cite stories of where they were when they heard that Kennedy was assassinated, our generation is full of September 11 stories. Do you have a September 11 story, Pete?

I have fabricated a story, over the years. It's easier that way. Otherwise, I'd have to go into involved explanations. That September I was so anaesthetised, moving through my days, in a haze of fatigue, that memories of my days have become indistinct and I do not have an authentic memory about what I was doing when I heard about the twin towers coming down on September 11, 2001.

In contrast, my memories of September 29, 2001 are agonizingly vivid and grittily techni-coloured. This will surprise you (because we both know how much I have always hated football), but I can tell you that Alastair Lynch scored the first goal of the match and that Brisbane won by a margin of twenty-six points- their first ever Australian Football League premiership win.

We walked to your Mum's that afternoon, past the town's distinctive weather-board houses. Did you notice that I had paired a pair of black pedal-pushers with a long-sleeved red tee, in support of your team, Essendon? Pushing the pram, you were pumped, whilst I walked at a more moderate pace with a three-year-old in tow, promising him we were almost there at every intersection.

At your mother's house, the choices were dire: tupperware talk in the newly renovated kitchen or watching football with the boys. I chose the latter.

Watching the A.F.L grand final, I remember sitting back and observing proceedings in the detached way you do, when everyone else is drinking alcohol and you're not. Braydon was terrified. He didn't know where to sit, his eyes kept flickering over to you, before he took something to eat or drink. He was so scared of messing up.

Up until then, I had taken some comfort in the fact that you were only hurting me. I prided myself on watching Braydon around you like a hawk; you two were never alone together. Up until then, I had even convinced myself that I had shielded my son sufficiently from our conflict that he was untouched by it. Watching my son's nervousness, while you and your brothers drank beer and loudly barked put-downs at the television, I felt a grim stillness settle upon me. Smiling politely at jokes, nodding, declining offers of beer, I like to think I maintained a veneer of calm inscrutability. But my inner voice was verging on hysteria,

'What the fuck has Pete done to him? How the fuck did he get to him?'

Your Mum, Catherine, the fundamentalist Christian tee-totaler dropped us off at home, so we wouldn't have to brave those country town side-walks in the dark (I know that sounds horribly bitchy, but writing about all this makes me feel entitled to as much mean-spiritedness as I can muster, Pete). When we got home, you were argumentative in that way that utterly intoxicated people can get, sometimes. You were frustrated with Braydon about something. To be honest, I don't even remember what it was anymore. You grabbed Braydon roughly by the arm, threw open the screen door and pointed to a washing basket outside.

'Stand in there, you cunt!' I tried to stop you, as Braydon went and did what he was told. My three-year-old son was dutifully compliant... just did what he was told. And I couldn't help but see it, then. Braydon was nearly four-years-old, but, already, he expected to be

treated badly. While I went groping for the screen door to get my son back inside, you grabbed me by the back of the red shirt I had chosen especially to show support for your football team and you threw me onto the mattress. Then, you got on top of me.

'Please, Pete, it's cold out there. You're drunk. You don't know what you're doing.' You pressed all your weight down on me.

'You want him back inside? Then, fuck me like you mean it!'

What could I do? I did. I felt like a desperate, dirty whore. Heroin had never reduced me to bartering fucking for favours, but you did, Pete.

That was the moment when I knew I had to leave you.

V

*

I didn't see it comin' when she left. I was at court. It was just a mention about when I'd assaulted her. I got home before twelve and the place was all locked up. There was a note on the door. It read:-

This isn't working out. I need to have a break from you.

I managed to break in. Clothes were gone.

Mum wanted me to go to Family Court. I just wanted 'er back. I rang 'er Mother, 'er son's grandmother, everybody I could think of. After three days, it paid off. She rang the flat.

'Please stop ringing my family and friends, Pete. I need some space. Please respect that.' She was tryin' to sound strong, but I knew if I kept 'er on the phone, there was a good chance I could talk 'er 'round.

'Are you 'n' Michael okay?' I asked 'er, real softly.

'We're fine,' she said. Still tryin' to sound staunch, but I knew 'er so well, ya know, mate, I could hear 'er waverin' a bit.

'Why, babe? How could you do this to us?' I asked. I was so desperate. I was in fuckin' tears, for fuck's sake. Mate, you got no idea how devastated I felt. I knew she could hear me cryin', but I wanted 'er to. I wanted 'er to know how cruel she was bein'.

'You can't do what you did to Braydon,' she said. Her voice was real cold. I knew exactly what she meant.

'It won't happen again, babe, I promise.'

She was talkun 'bout Grand Final Night. We had spent the day at Mum's. Okay, I'll admit it! I had too many beers. When we got home,

126

the kid pissed me off. I shouldna done what I done. I was so pissed I thought it was okay. I shouldna called him a cunt, but she hadda know I only did what I did 'coz I was drunk 'n' pissed off 'coz I lost money on me footy bets!

When I think back on it now, I shoulda known somethin' was off. The next day, she'd sent Braydon to stay with his Gran, Steve. She'd told me casually the next mornin',

'Braydon's going to stay with Sarah for a while because Sarah thinks we need some time alone with the baby.'

'Good,' I'd mumbled, hung-over. She'd fought so fucking hard for that kid! How did I not see it? She musta been plannin' to leave for the full week he was away.

'I can understand you doin' this to me, but what 'bout me Mum?' I asked 'er over the phone. I wanted 'er to feel guilty, 'Mum doesn't deserve this, babe.'

'I've got to go, now, Pete,' she said softly. I was cryin'. I couldn't believe this was how it was gunna end.

'Please don't hang up. What 'bout Michael? I've gotta see him, babe. Please!'

*

She stayed at a women's refuge for a coupla weeks. She'd stay over at 'er community housing flat sometimes, when Braydon wasn't with 'er (she had a few weeks left on the lease and she'd already pre-paid 'er rent). The sex was incredible every time. I was gentle with her. I kissed her eye-lids before I made love to her.

'I miss ya babe and I'll kill meself if you don't come back to me,' I told 'er, after we'd made love one night.

'Honey, please don't say that.' I held 'er tighter.

'It's true. I love you and I couldn't live without ya.'

One night, she got pretty heavy with me. She was lyin' on me chest. I couldn't see 'er face. Her voice was soft.

'Are you ever going to tell me?'

'Tell ya what?'

'Why you are this way.'

'What d'ya mean?' Her voice wasn't harsh or anythin'. She didn't sound like she was lordin' it over me or anythin'. She just said it real gentle, like she really wanted to understand,

'You hurt women and children, Pete. Who hurt you?'

D'ya still remember, Steve? Bein' little- when it got real loud? I can remember climbin' in the top bunk, slippin' under your doona with you. Don't worry, mate, I didn't go there. Never have. Not with 'er or anybody else… I just said,

'Does it matter? I know I gotta change, isn't that all that matters?'

The chick got under me skin, mate, I'll admit it. When we couldn't be together 'coz she 'ad her son with 'er, we chatted on the phone ev'ry night for 'bout an hour. I begged 'er to come home ev'ry night. If I could hear 'er voice for an hour ev'ry night, I was okay until the next time I saw her.

Otherwise, I'd get desperate! I'd ring up 'er mother's house and Sarah's house. She knew I'd do it. She didn't know what I'd say. With all the dirt I had on 'er, I coulda destroyed any chance she 'ad of keepin' the kids. So, she rang me ev'ry night like clock-work.

One night, she rang me up from the refuge.

'I'm pregnant,' she said, when I'd finished tellin' 'er 'bout me day. 'That's why Michael's not feeding. My breast milk's gone sour.'

'How?'

'I don't know. You're not supposed to be able to get pregnant, while you're breast-feeding. I guess I'm just particularly fertile.'

'Oh shit, I can't do this again! We'll have three kids under five, can you imagine it? We'll have to get married.' Me voice was desperate. She was quiet for a long time. I remembered 'er words, when she'd told me she was pregnant with Michael. How she didn't think an abortion was in 'er.

'I know what I need to do. I just need to get the money together.' I thought 'bout 'er killin' our child. She'd be killin' another Michael.

'No, babe, listen, I didn't mean it! I'll marry you! I love you, ya know. I wanna be with ya for the rest of me life.' Any other chick'd be flattered to be proposed to. She wasn't.

'No, Pete, it's not right to bring a child into the world, when we're going through all this. I'm having an abortion.' She didn't ask me. The bitch told me, like it 'ad nothin' to do me...

In November 2001, when me son was barely five months old, she aborted our second child. She had the abortion the day before she moved into 'er new place. She paid for it 'erself. I couldn't go with 'er, because I hadda be in court for the hearin' (you know, from when the police had charged me with assault, for chokin' her).

I got 'er to write a note, before she left that mornin' for 'er appointment,

I'm sorry. Keep Michael. I can't handle it. I don't know what got into me. Nothing happened. I should have never rung the police.

Me lawyer used it in me defence and to argue I was a single dad now. I got off. Later, I used the note in Family Court to discredit 'er as a mother.

I asked her if she was okay, afterwards,

'Some children aren't meant to be born and this was one of them.' Her eyes were so fucking cold, Steve. She was so hard, now, so tuff. She wasn't the same gullible, sweet chick I'd met sixteen months before, anymore. She scared me a little when her mouth was set like that. I promised 'er I'd never do anythin' bad to 'er son again. And I didn't. From that day on, Braydon was off limits.

'I'm gunna be a new man for you, babe,' I promised 'er.

I apologised to the little dweeb. Ate the biggest slice o' humble pie I ever 'ad to in me life.

'Braydon, what I did was wrong. I was drunk, but that doesn't make it okay. I am gunna try 'n' make it up to ya. Will you let me?' She waited. He nodded.

She took me back. I knew she would. A woman like that can't stand livin' alone. She needs to have someone, who worships 'er. I may have me faults, Steve, but she hadda know, no one was ever goin' to worship 'er like I did.

The refuge workers had helped her get a guvvy flat in the city. Sometimes, there were syringes in the walk-ways. Her neighbour was a loud drunk, who thumped the shit out of his kid, when he got too drunk. She told me she knew the place from when she'd been a junkie. It was one of the places, where she'd scored smack in the old days. No one had a job. People spent their days sittun 'round smokun pot or shootun up other harder drugs. At about the time she moved in, they were dumpin' a lotta ex-cons there when they got outta jail. Before that, they'd always parked those fellas in the guvvy flats on the south side, but those flats'd been pulled down...

She couldn't kid 'erself 'bout where she was livin' anymore. I could see it in 'er eyes. She'd thought she could get out by studyin'. Now, she hadda know better. Like I said, she was harder, somehow.

'Have nothing to do with these people,' she said real staunchly, 'If you want to score pot, don't do it here. It's simple, Pete. Don't shit where you eat.'

Letter 10

In Brief: Haemon Gill, 29, of Norlane appeared in court yesterday. Gill is on trial for the murder of his de-facto wife's two-year-old son, Lewis Jacob Blackley. Police found the child's body just before 10am on November 11, 2001 in his Norlane home, with his head trapped between a sofa cushion and the back of the sofa. It is alleged Gill battered the child to death.

Dear Pete,

The numbness spread like an ink-blot on napkin tissue, quickly becoming overwhelming. I had expected a radical, underground, feminist den, was surprised that the women's refuge was just a huge suburban house. Many of the rooms were communal—an almost industrial-sized kitchen, a dining table large enough to seat two football teams, a living room crowded with sofas and bean bags. My sanctuary was a lockable bed-room with enough bunk-bed room that I could have brought a tribe of four or five children. The quilt covers were bright blue and patterned and the curtains matched. On my first night there, Michael suckled reluctantly and I wondered if he was missing familiar surrounds.

The second night Braydon came to stay with us (I needn't have feared that Richard would balk at Braydon continuing to spend time with me. He and Sarah were extremely supportive of my decision to leave you...). My reunion with my son was an exhausting, exquisite parody of normality. I imagine Braydon detected the artifice in my frantic joviality. (Who was this woman, who looked like his mother, but spoke like one of the 'Wiggles'?) It was a strain to keep the frenzied meal-time chat about 'Bob the Builder' from sounding too forced.

Still moving as if through molasses, I took Sarah's call on the third day. Silly, chatty Sarah, straining to construct some normality out of a surreal conversation with her former daughter-in-law, who was living in a women's refuge, had the bad sense to tell me frankly,

'Pete rang last night. I almost felt sorry for him. He was in tears, telling me, "I just want to know Michael's okay". Of course, I didn't tell him *where you were. He said he'd keep ringing back. I just left the phone off the hook. So how's Braydon doing?'*

Sarah didn't understand you were just firing a warning shot. You weren't going to rest until you found me. Strangely, there was no panicked fluttering in my stomach. The resignation settled over me, as I made my first call to you from the refuge.

For the first time, each one of your pleas and all your heart-felt tears seemed so distant from me and, in my numbness, I had a strange sense of bewilderment- remembering that these were cues for me to forgive you, but feeling an almost amnesiac struggle to remember what I was supposed to do or say.

Resistance felt so futile. So, I dutifully rang you and listened, as you begged me to forgive you (the threat of the lengths you would go to if I didn't take you back was an under-current in every conversation). I met with you when I could (when Braydon was not with me). I had sex with you when you wanted me to. A part of me remembered the old tender responses to those remorseful, dark eyes but, without meaning to hurt you, Pete, sex that spring was pretty mechanical, for me.

This time a doctor told me I was pregnant (the 'alpha' women, who worked at that refuge surrounded me one afternoon in an ungainly 'intervention' of sorts. Worried about my depressed state, they insisted on a check-up). Telling you felt perfunctory. I didn't really hear your response. I knew what I had to do.

Like everything else, it was just a series of small steps. The first step was just a phone call. I wrote down an appointment time and directions.

I woke up a little anxious about the next step. To be honest, your thoughtless, desperate selfishness that morning was a relief. It was your hearing day, remember? I was risking a warrant by ignoring

the subpoena, but I didn't have the energy to resist you and, anyway, I had other plans, which were more important.

Your eyes were pleading and tear-filled. 'Please babe, just write to the court that you lied. Pretend you can't handle it, or something. They won't come after you, but, ya know they'll put me in jail.' You came up behind me, nibbled my neck. You were begging, 'Please.' Then your voice broke, 'I'll die if they send me to jail!' I scribbled the required lies neatly, succinctly and then went and showered.

You were gone by the time I walked to the bus-stop. Obsessed with your own trial that day, you'd forgotten about mine. The next step was paying my bus fare.

I followed my scribbled directions, when I got to to the city. I filled in the questionnaire. I lay down for the ultrasound and stared at the ceiling, while the cold gel was rubbed over my still flat stomach. I paid the receptionist $180.00 and flashed my Medicare and Health-care cards.

The nurse struggled to find a vein, as they always do (in my junkie days, I was not always fastidious about vein care). I resisted the urge to sit up on the gurney and offer the benefit of my expertise, 'Here, let me!' After some frustrated fumbling, she finally found a vein.

When I woke up, the receptionist checked I had transport home. 'I've booked a cab,' I said and walked downstairs to the street, where my cab was already waiting. I expected to feel sad. I didn't. By focusing on the mechanics of each small step, I silenced the doubt. At the end of the day, Pete, an abortion is just a series of steps.

My stay at the refuge ended the next day, when I moved into my new home. If I hadn't felt so numb, I might have smiled at the irony. The flat I was offered by the city's Housing Commission in that junkie hell-hole was, after all, just another massive 'fuck you!' from the universe.

137

As I unpacked boxes, I noted that there was a door at the end of my block that seemed to be knocked on, with fierce, insistent knocks, far too often. I decided that the tenant was an entrepreneur. I decided that there were worse career choices. After all, he was distributing a product, where demand would always exceed supply. He had no advertising over-heads. He could be a hands-on dad, working from home, which was probably a mixed blessing for the the two toddlers with identical, number two hair-cuts, whom I saw wandering around, runny-nosed with vegemite stains on their chins and on the collars of their faded T-shirts.

Carrying boxes up the stairwell from my storage space downstairs, I kept averting my eyes. Despite my efforts, I couldn't avoid eye contact with one of my neighbour's pale, skinny visitors. The pin-prick pupils were all the confirmation I needed to know what my entrepreneur neighbour's drug of choice was.

I spent my first night in my new home alone in my bed. I lay awake, listening to a neighbour yelling. The words were not clear enough to discern exactly, because of their slurred quality, but I could tell he was swearing. And here's the thing, Pete, as I fell asleep to the bleak sound-track of my new life, I knew in my gut I would take you back. The horror of what that would mean did not escape me. I just didn't care anymore.

V

I woulda thought a chick like that woulda gone running back to drugs in a place like that. For fuck's sake, she was livin' in the same flats, where 'er ex-dealer'd been dealin' before he was locked up! She didn't. She kept 'erself to 'erself. She kept tellin' me not to score pot there.

It was easy enough for her! She didn't hang out anymore for anythin'! She was doin' summer school at uni, tryin' to catch up so she could finish 'er law degree. I was stuck in the flat all day alone (the kids were both at day-care just up the road). I needed to score. I wasn't gunna catch a $1.70 bus outta the city and then catch a $1.70 bus back ev'ry time I hadda score $10.00 or $20.00 worth of pot. It was simple economics. She was always forkin' over money for me dope and whingin' 'bout it so I was doin' *her* a favour, really. I was savin' *her* money! It was worth scorin' off someone local.

So I dunno why she was so mad when she got home from uni that day, after she'd picked up the kids from day-care, and saw two strangers with a cask of wine sittin' in 'er flat. I could see in 'er eyes that she was furious with me. She dumped 'er backpack, sent Braydon to go and play with one of his mates for a bit, put Michael down with a bottle and looked at me. Her face was murderous.

'This is Crystal and Willy,' I said, takin' a deep suck of me bong. I dunno why she was so pissed off. They were both okay. Okay, Crystal was clearly a drug-fucked whore and you could tell, just by lookin' at Willy, that he done time, but why'd she have to be so judgemental? She was an ex-junkie, 'erself! And they'd brought over a cask of wine!

She looked at Crystal and I could tell what she was thinkin'. Anybody would. Crystal was a fucking thing, okay. She had too much peroxide in her bleached blonde hair, her mascara was caked on thick and she wore just fuckin' too much make-up. She had massive tits and wore clothes that were too tight 'n' skimpy.

She looked at Willy. Willy was an old ex-con. He was a wrinkled old thing with jail tatts all over 'is body. He'd spent more of 'is life in jail than out, but he was good value, mate. He'd shoplift lobster for the thrill of it so he could tell ya the story later. He hated lobster, but figured someone would buy it. He told amazun yarns- not just 'bout shopliftun lobster, but other stuff, too. He was always good for a laugh, you know- so I don't get why she was so pissed off.

She looked at me with 'er tight little mouth 'n' said,

'I'm making dinner. Who's staying?' Of course, they both put their hands up for a free meal. That's the thing 'bout people like that. They've been so rejected that they have no shame left. They will take anythin' they're offered and turn into an opportunity to screw you over, even if it's just by makin' ya feel uncomfortable. She didn't get it. I did.

I'll give him this. Willy knew how to play 'er. He pissed in 'er pocket all night, was extra nice to Braydon over dinner, he encouraged 'er to drink wine, while she waved it off.

'Wow, stayin' off smack. That's huge! You're a dark horse, aren't you? Just doing your thing, all quiet. Keeping to yourself, when this major shit's going on. Good onya!' She smiled. She was flattered, but she didn't buy his bull-shit. She made it clear all night she did not want them there.

Anyone could see Crystal comin' a mile off. She was someone to score off. She had pot. She sold it to buy speed and wine. She fucked whoever would have her when she was short. She was a fucking whore. Crystal was happy when she dragged people down to her level. She tried to crack onto me the first time I met 'er.

'You know Crystal asked me to fuck her while you were at uni today?' I told 'er when they'd both left. I dunno why I said it. I guess I just wanted to shift the heat off me. She was still fuming. Not my fault. They'd offered 'er wine 'n' pot. She was the one, who'd chosen not to be a part of it.

'Crystal wants to fuck anything in pants. You really shouldn't be putting *that one* on your resume,' she said real sarcastic. Her eyes were cold. Her voice was cool and she was slammin' things, as she did the washun up. It always gave me a hard on to see 'er jealous. I came up behind 'er and started nibblin' 'er neck.

'Why would I touch her when I have you?' She stiffened so I started playin' with 'er tits, rubbing me cock against 'er.

'This is how it all begins!' she said, pullin' away. 'Pretty soon, you'll have people injecting drugs in here. We've got children, for Christ's sake! I know what these people are like. I've been one of them, remember, Pete?' I put me hand under 'er shirt and began feelun 'er up.

'I know. You're right. I'm sorry.'

*

When I think back on it now, I know she was right, Steve. She was so fucking smart. She knew Crystal wanted to fuck me, so she set out to protect 'er turf. She was *so* nice to Crystal. She started laughing- no, not just laughing, cackling!- at Crystal's jokes. When Crystal brought over casks of wine, she drank one single glass of wine to be polite and then smiled 'n' listened while Crystal raved on and on, gettun drunker 'n' drunker. Crystal was a speed freak and she could talk real fast for hours 'bout shit.

'I don't wanna fuck you anymore. Your missus is *too* fucking nice,' Crystal told me a month into the piece. The missus was at uni. I'd thought Crystal had come over to put 'er money where 'er mouth was. She hadn't and I sucked up the disappointment 'n' nodded. Crystal knew her words would get back to me missus and then their deal would be sealed.

She mighta been smart, but she was still clueless about some things. She didn't know how to handle the world she was livin' in now. I'll never forget the time she nearly got 'erself killed 'coz she was too fucking thick to know what she was saying.

We were drinking with a room full of fellas. They were celebratin' 'coz one of 'em had just got out after doin' a three-year stretch. They were talkun 'bout dogs. Those fellas had brought over some wicked pot and we were supposed to be bein' good hosts. She'd already put them off-side 'coz she wouldn't smoke their pot or drink any of their booze. Her comment wasn't just dangerous. It was rude. It was bad hospitality, for fuck's sake!

'Yeah, dogs are the fucking lowest form of life. Cops have tried to make me rat a bunch of times, but I wouldn't do it,' said Duncan, the drunk hard-ass, who lived next door. He sucked on the bong and passed it on. Everyone started mumblin' in agreement. She hadda play fucking devil's advocate, didn't she? Lord it over everybody, in her fucking posh, superior voice.

'I'm sorry, but, if it comes down to me and my children, and I have to inform on you to stay out of jail, then I'm going to do it.' The room went cold. Stupid bitch! It was all right for her. I was the one, who was gunna get smashed tryin' to defend 'er…

Look, she was absolutely right. I'd ratted on Gazza to stay out of jail, by then, and I've ratted on half a dozen other guys, since. Everybody

142

rats when they need to, but you never fucking admit it! I have no doubt half of those fellas had been the chattiest dogs on the face o' the earth, when it suited them. But, you always pretend it's a low-life act that you'd never be a part of. It's an unwritten rule. You just don't say that shit *out loud*. The bitch was so thick she didn't get it.

Crystal broke the ice by laughing. Crystal saved her fucking life that night! I made sure she would never do somethin' so stupid again, when they left.

*

I reckon Crystal found her funny 'n' interestin'. That's why she was over all the time with wine. Crystal was desperate for a friend. Pretty soon, me missus was scoring speed with her on pay-day.

Don't get me wrong, Steve. The missus wasn't a junkie. She was very disciplined, like that. She'd pay her rent, the phone and electricity bill over the phone. She'd put aside nuff cash for a bus pass and 'er day-care fees. She'd do two weeks' food shoppin' and then put aside a bitta cash for me, in case I was hanging out for weed later in the week and then she'd score a single point of speed. She'd use the extra hours she was awake, while the kids were away, to study. Somehow, she still had nuff left over for wine or port on the days, when Crystal didn't bring any over, so I could get drunk. I'll give 'er this. The bitch knew how to budget.

She tried to convince me not to go ahead with it, Steve.

'Honestly, Pete, you hate needles! Why do you want to do this? If you want to try speed, you can just smoke it, you know!'

'I wanna know what it's like. Ya know if you're not gunna do it, Crystal will.' I knew that'd change 'er mind. Crystal was a wild fuckin' bitch 'n' there was no tellun what she'd do. She sighed 'n' then she

143

taught me 'ow to inject meself with speed. I know you hate needles, but it was such a mad rush, mate, and I'd picked up the hang of it, by the second time... I knew from the first time I'd be doin' it again.

*

We'd shot up some speed that Saturdee. We'd been up all night playin' Monopoly, after she'd finished crammin' for her exams. We were havin' that slow, sleepy Sundee mornin' sex, you know. She was ridun me cock when I saw 'er face. Her expression was one of pure shock. She was pantin' furiously, fucking hard. She'd closed her eyes and suddenly they shot open. The look on 'er face was incredible. That's when she told me she'd come for the first time.

After that, she wanted it desperately and so did I. If she'd been great in bed before, she was incredible now that she couldn't get enough. She'd go off like a frog in a sock. Sometimes, I'd just watch her, fingerin' 'erself until I was ready. She'd come in seconds, sometimes. She was so fucking sexy. On pay day, when we were revvin' on speed, the orgasms were even more incredible.

I loved watchin' her come, but, sometimes, just to mix it up a bit, I'd stop when I could feel she was on the brink- just so I could look at that face. I wish I coulda freeze-framed it- that look, as her face got desperate. You could just tell she'd do anythin' in that moment to get me goin' inside her again. I loved that feelin' I'd get when her face got desperate like that. That look made me feel ten-feet tall, like I just snorted coke, like the king of the world...

*

The same month she got 'er summer school grades (Fuck knows how she did it, but she passed!) and started her first Autumn semester at uni, I was charged with assault again. The newspapers made out I'd beat her over any little thing. I didn't. She'd let one of the neighbours take

144

Michael for a play date! She's the one, who'd warned me 'bout these people. What the fuck was she thinkin' bringing them into our home and letting one of them take Michael and *her* Braydon to the park?

I was pretty drunk, but I know I went too far that time. The back of 'er head was mushy in me hands when I was finished with 'er, but we were startin' over. What was she thinkin' talkun to the cops? With the kinda damage I done to her, I coulda gotten some serious time! What the fuck was she thinkin'? The cop had cornered 'er when she left the flat to go 'n' get the boys back. The cops'd been called by some guy, who'd been bashed in the phone box at the end of the street.

The cops were sneaky as. She told me later that she never woulda made a statement if the cops hadn't told her I'd bashed the poor guy in the phone box and that they were chargin' me with assault anyway.

'I've stopped caring what you do to me, Pete, but you cannot just bash some poor guy's brains in, because you're drunk.'

She was right, Steve. I don't blame her for what she did. I would never talk to the police 'bout her hittin' me, but if she hit you or some poor, defenceless guy on the street, then I think I woulda made a statement, too. So, I can understand where she was comin' from. It just so happened that this time she was wrong. I hadn't bashed the guy up. In the end, I only got a fine. The blood on me shirt was hers not his. Their case fell apart, but it took almost a full year 'n' fuck knows how many goddamned court dates before that came to pass.

When I got released on bail after they'd processed me for bashin' her head in, I told meself, 'This is over.' They'd charged me after talkun to her. Me shirt was covered in 'er blood when they nabbed me and charged me with two counts of assault- one on her, one on the guy in the phone box.

After I rang Mum to come 'n' pick me up, I rang 'er to tell her I was comin' to get me son.

'I'm on me way with Mum. Don't you dare call the police, d'ya hear me, bitch?'

That woulda been it. I had me son back in me arms, a backpack of clothes on me back. She knew I wasn't comin' back. She kissed me on the mouth- open-mouthed. It was the sexiest kiss of me fucking life.

'You're bringing him back tomorrow.' She looked me in the eye and rubbed the back of her head real casually. She knew *only* I'd know the threat in that. I knew I'd be back and I was.

She tried to hold out for a bit, clampin' her legs together in the mornin'. I told her how sorry I was,

'I know I did wrong. When I felt the back of your head, it was soft and mooshy and I was so scared about what I done,' I was in tears, for fuck's sake, if you can imagine it, 'but babe, don't let them put me in jail please.' She kissed away me tears, pulled her legs apart. I rammed meself so hard into her. She was squealin' in pain. It was amazun.

I'll give her this. She was smart. She could work out the angles on a problem and she did good. She conned a letter outta her doctor sayun she was experiencing severe post-natal depression. I gave it to me lawyer to get me off. Later, both Mum and me used it to crucify her in Family Court.

*

I didn't enjoy hitting her. I hated lookun at her face in the mornin', when I couldn't control meself and I left bruises behind. It made me 'shamed, but she was honestly so unbearable, to me, when I was

146

drinkin' and I had mates 'round. It was like I'd see her clearly, for the first time, when other people were around.

At first she tried ignorin' me 'n' my mates. She'd lock 'erself in 'er room to study. I told 'er how rude it was.

'You make me feel like ya don't want me 'n' me mates around.'

'Pete, these aren't your mates. These are free-loaders, who bring over beer and cask wine so that they can pester you for cones all week,' she said. 'I actually *don't* want them around.'

'Can't you just try for me, babe? It's all right for you. You gotta life outside this flat. You're goin' to uni. I 'ave to hang 'round here all day. Besides when I'm short, they help me out too with cones 'n' stuff.' She sighed. She was pissed off 'bout it, but she started makin' an effort.

Careful whatcha wish for, Steve! I think it was worse when she started makin' the effort. Crystal knew I couldn't say no (she was me connection!). She brought free-loaders 'round ev'ry weekend. Crystal'd fucked everyone and had no sellun power left. So, Crystal'd bring over ev'ry man and his dog to meet me beautiful girlfriend. Crystal'd try 'n' get her to drink wine.

Me missus stayed sober. She could get lippy and I'll give her this, other people found her very funny (I never saw it meself!).

Other times, when Crystal brought over fellas she was fuckin' that week, the missus just sat there, with a diet coke, laughin' on the other side of the room. She would get into a conversation with some guy (one o' Crystal's latest fucks) who was revvin' off 'is head on speed. She'd talk for hours. I hated it.

I'd watch her, while I skulled beer. I'd stagger over ev'ry once in a while to kiss her and mark me territory. Afterwards, she'd make fun of the poor guy. She'd recount his stupid words word-for-word and accent perfect too.

'Yeah, there's nuthin wrong with jail, mate. Free feed, free roof over ya head, no 'lectrickery to pay.' She was imitatin' some free-loader, who'd been over with Crystal. 'Fucking moron!' she said, as she cleaned up the empty beer bottles 'n' shit. It pissed me off. This was me world 'n' she was makin' fun of it: like she was better than this.

She thought she was so smart, but she was still clueless 'bout everythin' goin' on. She didn't cotton on why Crystal was over all the time with wine 'n' men. Crystal wanted to pimp me missus for drugs. I knew it. Crystal knew I knew it. Only me stupid bitch of a girlfriend couldn't see it. She didn't get that, when she made time to talk to the free-loaders and speed freaks, they were just weighin' up 'ow good a fuck she'd be. She was leadin' 'em on Steve and you know I couldn't let her get away with *that*...

After I'd finished with 'er, I heard 'er talkun to Crystal on the phone,

'Honey, it's probably better if you spend the weekends somewhere else, from now on. I've got heaps of studying to catch up on over the next few weeks, okay?' Her eye was swollen shut. She hung up and fumbled 'round lookin' for sunglasses so she could take the boys to day-care.

I'll give Crystal this. Crystal stopped bringin' the free-loaders 'round, but she couldn't stay away. I hated Crystal. She was me pot connection and I needed her to hang 'round sometimes, but she fucking pushed the friendship. Crystal would come and whip me missus off to the club, sometimes.

Mate, me missus could be a stupid, bleedun hearted bitch 'n' there were some things in the world she just couldn't let go of, ya know. We fought about Crystal all the time.

'Look, I know she's fucked-up, but she's doing what she needs to do to survive. You have no idea the horrendous life that woman has had. The fact that she gets up every morning is a miracle, in itself! If she were a man, screwing around, we wouldn't be having this argument,' she said.

'Don't you get it? If she was a man, she wouldn't be a mum, but she is! She *is*, god damn it! She's got four fucking kids –you've seen them, for fuck's sake; they've stayed over, when she was too busy fucking to feed 'em. You know 'ow fucked those kids are and it's all down to 'er. How can you *not* get that?'

'But, that's her. Not me.'

'It *is* you when you're with 'er!'

'That's not fair, Pete,' she said. She was firm, when she spoke, 'Just because I don't judge her doesn't mean I want to *be* like her!'

'Well, what d'ya do down at the club when you take off?'

'Nothing, Pete. I keep her company. I make her laugh. Sometimes, I'll have a beer. Sometimes, I'll stop her from doing something stupid she might regret later. Sometimes, I can't. We talk about girl stuff, that's all.'

'Yeah, right!'

Crystal loved her. Crystal had never had a friend, who didn't judge her. Crystal was devoted, as much as Crystal could be. Crystal ripped into me a few times, when she saw the bruises, but she still took me money. She still sold me weed.

Me stupid feminist girlfriend thought there was somethin' noble in whorin' yourself. That Women's Studies course must have turned her brain a bit soft, I dunno. She was just so fucking thick sometimes.

149

I dunno what she got out of being friends with Crystal, but I reckon it was more of that bleedun heart bull-shit. She needed to feel needed. At one point, she was holdin' onto Crystal's A.T.M. card so Crystal wouldn't blow her pay at the club. At three a.m., she'd walk down and get Crystal to take out enough cash to feed her four kids (before Crystal hit the pokies) and she'd hold onto the cash until the next day and take Crystal food shoppun.

One night, Crystal came over late. She'd been revvin' on speed for days. Crystal was talkun shit, but it was scary, suicidal talk. I wanted Crystal to leave. Crystal was freakin' me out and ruining me high. Me missus just talked to her calm as, got her to sleep on the sofa. 'She'll be okay in the morning,' she whispered.

Maybe, that's what she got outta bein' friends with Crystal. She just needed to be able to look after someone 'n' be good at it. She sure as hell couldn't handle the kids. That's why she sent them off to day-care, while she was at uni! She sure as hell couldn't look after 'erself. You only hadda look at her bruised body to know that!

But maybe it was really another one of her crazy head-games and she never *really* liked Crystal. Maybe, she knew she was gunna use Crystal from the start. The bitch was smart enough 'n' twisted enough that I can see her doin' that.

Letter 11

In Brief: Glenn William Eaglesham, 33, was sentenced today after being convicted recently of murdering his wife, Petrina Joy Eaglesham on March 11, 2002. Petrina was discovered in a car, with her throat slashed. Petrina's diary revealed that Eaglesham had threatened her with a meat cleaver several days before murdering her.

Dear Pete,

Do you know that the stories of resistance still fascinate me? One of my clients deliberately nagged her husband the minute he got home from work. She routinely burnt his dinner. Inducing the beatings before he started drinking kept her alive. Another woman would call a time-out before her partner was going to hit her; just enough time to walk to the corner shop and grab some cigarettes. The rule was that he could 'go for broke' after she 'had a ciggie'. Sometimes, in the time it took her to walk to the corner shop and back and slowly smoke that first Marlboro red, he was able to contain his rage.

When jaded police officers ask, 'Why the hell doesn't she leave him?' I resist the urge to educate them. Staying alive, until the time is right, is a form of resistance after all, but my breath would be wasted explaining.

In a life, where the unthinkable becomes routine, resistance is a myriad of tiny acts of subversiveness cobbled together. So, I enrolled in Summer School (Administrative Law and Advanced Torts) and held my breath when I told you, waiting...

Then, I enrolled Braydon and Michael in that child-care centre down the street, remember Pete? And, although we both knew it was because there was no way I would be able to concentrate on lectures if either of my sons were in your care, there was no retaliation.

The apathy was the hardest to resist. When the alarm clock went off each morning, it took a mammoth act of will to shut out that inner voice (it sounded like yours, in my mind), 'Why ya botherin' with *all this? You know it's pointless. Ya never gunna make it through ya degree. Ya never gonna get outta here.'*

Having my shower, I washed away the inclination to give in to that voice and abandon my plans for the day and pop down to the end of my block and knock on that *door. By the time crusts were cut off sandwiches and bananas were fished out of pantries and packed into vibrantly coloured lunch-boxes, I was always running late.*

Racing down the street each morning with Braydon holding onto the stroller, squinting away icy morning breezes, I found myself waiting for the day when the ritual would snuff out the despair. That first walk of the day became as desperate as prayer.

Gradually, though, I found relief. Most mornings, by the time I boarded the bus to university, I was on a roll. The feeling of self-conscious resistance was gone by the time I was in class. I could focus on the first lecture of the day, without remembering that my life at home was lived so discordantly from this one.

On good days, I could even tolerate the indulgent idealism of those fresh-faced students, spruiking Green Left Weekly *and calling out socialist slogans in their long woollen army coats (army coats were the height of radical chic, in those days). On bad days, when the air of poverty hung over me no matter how carefully I dressed, I resented these prosperous weekend warriors, romanticising the plight of poverty, as if there was something noble about my life.*

I am so grateful we found Crystal. You never understood this and, now, on the pages you will never read, I can attempt an explanation.

The first time I met her, Crystal wore her promiscuity on her sleeve, like other people wear their hearts. She was stereo-typical in her hooker chic (remember the peroxide, the mascara, the short, tight denim skirt

and the knee-high boots?) I knew she'd tried to seduce you, even before you made that clumsy confession, at the sink that night.

Crystal spent so much time speeding and drinking, cackling and she was so heart-breakingly bawdy, (Was it you, who coined the term, "the life of the party, mate!"?) that her sadness was easy to miss. I saw the truth the second time I was in the same room as her, while she skulled a mug of fruity lexia, from a cask of wine. I don't know how I knew to ask her, but when you left the room, I blurted,

'How old were you?' Pete, she knew what I was asking. I could see it in her eyes. In the years since I left you I have learnt that there is some-times a code amongst survivors that transcends words, but I felt it for the first time with Crystal.

'Nine,' she said, in reply to my question.

'Your father?'

'No, my uncle. It felt good when he stroked me. It didn't hurt until later.' Pete, you were coming back into the room, by then, so she put on the mask again. 'But hon, isn't that always the way? Feels fucking good, until it doesn't and then he's fucking too far gone to care!' We both cackled and I reached out for her hand and squeezed it. You missed the gesture, too pre occupied with filling a mug with cheap wine.

In her teens, Crystal re-invented herself as a tart. She drew a line in the sand. No one can steal what you give away freely.

Here's the thing, Pete... Crystal made me feel guilty about my self-pity. Wallowing seemed so selfish. So, inspired by the brazen, broken, bot-tle-blonde, who sometimes walked three blocks to the highway when she was drunk and flashed her breasts at passing truckers, while she

howled at the moon, I decided to master the law. If I mastered the legal system, no one could use it to take my children away from me again.

Maybe, you sensed something that summer. You always felt enraged by things you could not understand. So, you thwarted my plans for studious seclusion by gathering free-loaders in my living room. And, just as you had felt compelled to piss on my essay, you had to fuck my friend.

Still, the zeal of my resistance burnt strongly (It was such a relief after the numbness of spring!). The first time I stared in the mirror and wondered how I would brave an Admin tutorial, with a cracked lip and a swollen eye, I heard Crystal's voice in my mind, howling at the moon, 'Fuck yas all!' And, so armed with foundation in my backpack and Polaroid sunglasses, I refused to skip school. It was my line in the sand.

Sometimes, I found sanctuary in the university's computer labs late at night. Dreading the thought of catching the bus home to you, I found solace, where the only sound was that of my fingers tapping keys on the key-board. Researching case law on legal data-bases, I felt safe and smart and free (all the things I wasn't anymore). I never held my breath in those quiet, studious hours before dawn and the freedom of breathing deeply was (almost) worth the reprisals I faced for being so late when I got home to you.

In March, the set-backs were an onslaught. First, Rosie died. Remember the cute, blue-eyed, blonde toddler, who seemed to wander ethereally down walk-ways littered with syringes, avoiding each one as if she were charmed, day-dreaming and singing 'twinkle twinkle little star'? They say her mother hadn't slept in thirty-six hours, when she got behind the wheel, but, then again, Pete, we both know the amphetamines were particularly potent that year...

156

And then there was the morning I faced that brown stain on the white bricks of my kitchen wall. I always told you that those bloody remnants from the back of my head wouldn't come off. I lied, Pete. (You were never going to grab steel wool and try your hand at scrubbing it off, after all). The symbolism was surely over-kill, by then, but every time I saw that brown blemish, I was reminded of how close you'd come to killing me.

In desperation, I sought out other acts of inadequate resistance. Each time I drove myself to exhaustion with amphetamine-induced studying or submitted to the release of orgasms that made me feel like a whore (you even appropriated the primal pleasure of my orgasms, Pete, each time you spat 'bitch' into my face when I was on the verge of coming), a part of me wished someone would hear the inner screams I could not voice. Then, maybe, all of it could just... stop.

Today, when I hear the stories of the dysfunctional resistance of abused women, who have turned to alcohol or promiscuity or who have started returning the violence, the sadness is almost unbearable. The police officers will never understand that the acts of defiance are always too much and never enough. No amount of resistance will ever make him change.

So, I wrestle with this quiet certainty: Pete, I am never going to understand why this happened to me, am I? Still, sitting here before dawn, I feel compelled to try.

V

*

In March 2002, the same month I was charged with assault for bashin' her head in, a two-year-old girl died in a car accident. Her mother survived the crash and tried to resuscitate her but the toddler had died by the time ambulance officers arrived.

The little girl spent weekends in one of our neighbour's flats with 'er father. It was hard to score dope for a couple of days. Everyone was so devastated.

The last lotta bruisin' on 'er face was still fadun. She hadda pack on make-up to go to the funeral.

'Her coffin was so small,' she said, afterwards. Her eyes were red-raw from cryin'. I hadn't gone to the funeral. Me bail conditions said I wasn't supposed to come near 'er. I was scared I might get nabbed. Plus, I didn't really see the point. Me bein' there wasn't gunna bring the kid back.

'Can you imagine if somethin' like that happened to Michael?' I asked her. 'It would kill *you*, wouldn't it?' She looked at me hard. She knew what I was hinting at. Look, mate, you've gotta know, I'd never do anythin' to me son. But dealin' with that crazy bitch was 'bout constantly keepin' 'er on 'er toes, if you know what I mean.

'It would kill us *both*, Pete.' Her face was cold. She looked at me steady. She wasn't tryin' to be subtle, either. She was lettin' me know if I ever let somethin' like that happen to our child, she'd find a way to kill me. I wished I'd remembered that conversation, Steve. Maybe I wouldn't be in 'ere, if I had.

*

I know now why she did what she did and I don't hate her for it. At the time, I didn't have a clue, but, like I said, Steve, I've had a lotta time to think.

She wanted to test us. I guess she thought in her crazy head, 'I will do anything for this guy, the sex is incredible. Is he worth it? Does he love me that much?' I coulda told her I loved her more than life itself. I guess she just needed to prove it to 'erself.

Crystal came over while she was at uni. Crystal told me the missus'd said it was okay. Crystal said the words, without skippin' a beat. She looked me in the eye. I believed her.

'Your missus said it's fine for you to fuck me.' Crystal had these huge tits. She went 'round braless sometimes and you just knew Crystal'd do anythin' without gettin' precious 'bout it.

I got Crystal to suck me off. I pushed her head hard into me cock. The missus woulda never let me do that to her so I did it with Crystal, instead. I fucked Crystal with a condom, 'coz I knew me missus worried 'bout S.T.D.'s. I thought I was bein' considerate 'bout it. I honestly thought that she'd said it was okay. I believed Crystal when Crystal said *she'd* be fine with it.

Well, she wasn't okay with it. When she got home from uni, she looked at me with the filthiest look. She knew. You'd better believe that the cutlery and crockery were bein' smashed somethin' chronic that night, while she cooked dinner and did the washun up. I tried to bring up the subject.

'Not now. I'll talk to you about this when the children are in bed,' she said in that tight, posh voice.

After she'd read him his story and put Braydon to bed, I asked her why she was takin' it out on me and not Crystal.

'Crystal told me you wanted us to do it!' I said desperate.

'Oh, come on, Pete! She said *that* and you believed her? I really get a kick out of Crystal and she's had a horrendous life, but we both know she's a whore. I don't expect a thing from her. She does what she needs to do to survive. She's not attached... she can fuck anyone she wants to for a schooner of beer. What hurts, Pete, is that I believed you were better than that.' The way she said it sounded real final.

'I'm sorry, babe, but I'm glad I did it. Now I know how good it is with you. You know, she just lies there. Not like you babe.'

I found out years later, she'd told Crystal to throw 'erself at me, told 'er just what to say. That's what I mean. She was fucking smart, but she was so fucking cold. Crystal thought she was her friend and she just used her like that.

She didn't think I'd go through with it, ya know, but she needed to prove it to 'erself. She didn't care who she hurt. It was entrapment, mate, but in her warped head, I'd failed her. She needed to know that I'd be faithful. She could put up with the beatings, so long as I didn't touch her son. She could hang in there and love me un-fucking-conditionally, so long as I was faithful. When she found out I wasn't, she didn't know why she was doin' it anymore.

*

After that, she got completely outta control. She sent Braydon off to his Gran's for the weekend ev'ry Fridee and I'd take Michael to spend the weekends with me Mum. It was like she didn't want the kids around so she could get up to no good. She stopped wantin' to spend time with me on the weekends. She'd say she was goin' to the library to study, but I never believed her.

I bet you anythin', when she said she was out studyin' all night at the uni computers, she was actually spendin' time with her junkie neighbours. I'm sure she spent her time drinkin' quickly and gettun drunk.

I guarantee you man, when she said she was crammin' at uni all night for an exam, she was actually passin' out on someone's floor. I bet you anythin' she woke up with carpet burn and no idea, who'd fucked her. She was that much of a fucking clueless slut, mate. She couldn't spend time with those people, without them taking advantage of 'er.

When she came home Sundee mornin's on the bus and claimed to've been studyin' all night, I never believed 'er. I beat her black 'n' blue a coupla times, but she never confessed what she really been up to. She was a stubborn bitch, like that, but I made me point. She stopped goin' to uni on the weekends and started studyin' at home. It wasn't easy for her 'coz of all the noise those fuckin' neighbours made, but I got to keep me eye on her.

One night, she was up studying at home, after the kids were asleep and Crystal came 'n' told me that she was takin' her out. Crystal didn't ask me, she told me. I couldn't say no in front of Crystal (she was me fucking connection!). So, she took off with Crystal, leaving me with the kids for the night. What kinda mother does that?!

She organised more and more sleepovers for Braydon and spent more and more nights ignorin' me while she was studyin'. Fuck that pissed me off Steve!

I tried to beat it outta her. It was like that was the only way I had left to make her pay me some fucking attention, mate!

Like I said, she was outta control. She kept makun me feel like I was not important to 'er anymore. She was always busy studyin' or at uni or pickun up the kids or makun dinner and washun up. She kept tellin' me She was too tired for sex. It was like I wasn't a parta her life anymore. You can't do that to someone you're gunna spend the resta ya life with! I beat her harder and only made meself feel worse.

*

Steve, I know they say it's never okay to beat a woman. I've said that meself, at times. But there's gotta be a line, doesn't there? When your girlfriend's a whore and a manipulative, crazy bitch and you wanna spend the resta ya life with her and she treats you like shit 'n' ignores you, it's not the same as just beating a woman up because you don't like what she cooked for dinner.

I don't think you can be a stuck-up slut and claim the high moral ground, 'coz your fella bashed you a couple of times. Am I wrong, mate?

Letter 12

Local News, 1 June 2002

A Serbian man was convicted of murdering his wife yesterday. Madraj Stojkovic, 48, claimed he acted in self-defence when he repeatedly struck his wife Vesna, 34, over the head with a hammer.

Dear Pete,

*I*n my post-Pete life, I make a big deal out of the boys' birthdays, Christmas and Easter. When our son turned four-years-old, he came home from pre-school to find the house in darkness. Holding his hand tightly, my palm was sweaty. My voice was shaking with anticipation, as I told him,

'Don't be scared. We just have to walk to that light over there.' Tentatively, we walked towards the only lit room in the house. Behind the door, was Michael's very first bike, decorated with streamers and balloons. I think I was more excited than he was, but I could almost hear his rapidly beating heart. (He was shell-shocked, but the cake helped him recover and, as he ate it, he kept questioning me a little cautiously to make sure that the exquisite bit of machinery was really all his – 'So, Mummy, I get to ride it, but Braydon doesn't?').

My habit for celebration began during our time together, Pete. Do you remember our only Easter in those dismal flats? I rallied together Crystal and a couple of other single mothers living at the complex. I bought rubber gloves and collected a dozen yellow syringe containers from the needle exchange service. First, we cleared the walk-ways of syringes. I felt a pang, thinking of little Rosie as we started the task, but for twenty-four hours, even the stone-cold junkies honoured our gift to our children.

Crystal and I collected donations from the other mums and went on a cackling shopping spree, buying mountains of Easter eggs and foil-wrapped bunnies. On Saturday night, we buried them throughout the complex.

:h inside_Updated.indd   165   3/31/2012   7:24:32 PM

Braydon, Michael and I had our first ever Easter egg hunt that Easter Sunday. It has become a family tradition. (In the garden of the house I live in now, there have been times when the Easter egg hunt has lasted until early afternoon. By then, chocolate eggs and foil-wrapped bunnies are melting in the April sun). Sadly, I think this was the last year. The boys are too old to believe in the Easter Bunny and the tradition feels a little hollow.

I bought many disposable cameras that autumn and took countless photographs of Braydon and Michael at that suburban park down the road (when I look at those photographs, now, I try to cling to those moments, again, and hope these narrow windows of relief from the bleakness have been enough to insulate my sons). You were still on your best behaviour with Braydon and I'll give you this, Pete... you seemed to genuinely adore our son. Sometimes, rubbing 'Deep Heat' into my wounds, that trade-off seemed sufficient.

But, there are some things I can't forgive you for, Pete. Michael's first birthday is one of them.

When I pictured that day in my mind, I never imagined myself drinking port. I dreamt of watching Michael opening presents, being more enchanted with the wrapping paper than the contents. I pictured Braydon drinking too much coke and myself wiping chocolate icing off Michael's chin and taking photos of him in his card-board party hat.

When Sarah came by and picked up Braydon for the rest of the weekend, I couldn't get her out the door fast enough. She had brought Michael a birthday present and she wanted to chat. I really wasn't in the mood, but I think I pulled off the polite pretence.

'So where's the birthday boy?' I didn't tell her I had no idea.

'He should be back any minute,' I said, trying to keep the tension out of my voice.

'Oh, I'm sorry I missed him!' she said. She looked genuinely sad that she had.

'Oh, well, I'll make sure he knows this present is from you.'

'Have a great day, darling. There's nothing like first birthdays, is there?' She smiled. Her eyes were reminiscent, 'it goes so quickly, doesn't it? They grow up so fast, don't they?' She chuckled and I attempted a smile. I think she finally sensed my eagerness for her to leave.

'Okay, well, then, you'll pick Braydon up from child-care Monday and I'll see you next week.'

'Yes! Bye Braydon, have a good time!' I said, trying to keep my voice natural, as I waved goodbye to him. I remembered my manners, with my hand on the door-knob. 'Thanks, again, for the present, Sarah.'

When you left the day before Michael's birthday, I was going through a shopping list of things I needed for my son's birthday. You pecked my cheek and said, 'I'll see ya tomorrow. Mum wants to do 'is birth-dee dinner tonight, so I'll crash there, okay, babe.' Steve was parked downstairs waiting for you. Steve beeped his horn and you bundled up Michael and his nappy bag and raced down the stairs.

Do you remember that your Mum's phone was disconnected, at that time? As the hours passed, I rang hospitals to eliminate the almost wistful fantasy of a car accident.

When I knew the wait was futile, I sat, cross-legged on my lounge-room floor in the dark, surrounded by wrapped birthday presents. There was a chocolate birthday cake in the fridge with a big wax, number one-shaped candle and there was a disposable camera on the bench. I drained a bottle of port. I dispensed with a glass and drank the sickly sweet liquid straight from the bottle. When Crystal came by, I ignored her knocking.

167

Pete, the day our son turned one, I spent the day wondering if you were ever bringing him back. I have made a point of making every birthday since that time special. As the boys grow out of childish wonder, those memories grow increasingly precious. There will always be one memory that is missing from the deck of birthday card memories and, for that, I will never forgive you.

V

*

When Mum had Michael's first birthdee party in June, she wasn't invited. By then, none of the family wanted her around, remember?

I coulda told 'er, but I didn't 'ave the guts to face 'er, so I took Michael to Mum's for a visit the day before and pretended I was gunna be back at her place for Michael's birthdee. We celebrated Michael's birthdee without 'is mother. Mum's phone was cut off at the time. There'd been no way for her to contact us.

She was annihilated on port 'n' cryin', when I got home the mornin' after Michael's birthdee. I'd never seen 'er drunk before.

'How could you do this? It was his *first* birthday and you took him the day before and didn't come back until now.' I held her. She was bawlin' 'er eyes out, 'I didn't know if you were coming back!' I actually felt pretty bad for her, but now she knew what it'd been like for me when she'd taken off to the women's refuge.

'This was the earliest I could get a lift, babe,' I lied, 'I'm sorry.' She was cryin' hard now, in that way drunk women do, that's real hardcore sad.

'You've won, Pete. You've proven that you were always right, from the start. *I* was the one, who was always fucked-up. No wonder you hit me. Look, at me, I can't even control myself for one night, when something unfortunate happens. I'm drunk! I'm clearly so fucked-up that I don't deserve to spend my son's first birthday with him. What else is there left to take from me, Pete? What other way can you punish me for being so fucked-up?' I held her, kissed the top of 'er head.

'You know that's not true,' I said. 'You're a good Mum and you study hard. You don't drink, for Michael's sake, even when I do. You have bad taste in mates, but I won't hold it against you.' I laughed, said it light. I wanted to break the tension. It didn't work.

'Then why did you do it?' She was drunk, but I could see it clear as in 'er eyes. She was heart-broken.

*

Look, I felt bad 'bout it, but, Steve, ya have no idea low she sank, while we were livin' together in those guvvy flats! If she was messy before, she was a down-right slob now. There was always washun to fold all over the place. There'd always be papers from 'er studyin' all over the dinin' table.

Plus, she was a fuckin' slut. Crystal put it sweet, mate, when she told me years later,

'Lloydee, you're better off without her, mate. Look, I know what people think of me,' Crystal said. She smiled. One thing I'll give Crystal is this. The chick was straight up, not pretentious, in the least, 'I'm a fat slutty chick, who'll do anything for a schooner, but I wasn't attached. Michael was a baby. You adored her, what the fuck was she thinking?'

'What d'ya mean?'

Crystal told me about the time we'd fucked each other, how the missus had told her just what to say...

'That's what I mean, Lloydee... she just used people, all the time. I may be a slut, mate, but at least with *me*, what you see is what you get... she was just all 'bout head games.'

170

Crystal 'n' me shagged for old times sake. Crystal was always up for sex. I was feelun horny and she'd offered, so why not? I gotta hand it to Crystal. There's nothin' that slut wouldn't do in bed, but it didn't matter. She was an even worse lay than I remembered.

*

I knew that July somethin' was comin' to a head. She was gettin' more 'n' more outta control. Steve, she couldn't keep her fucking mouth shut. She'd have to get lippy. She'd have a single drink and then get real brave. She'd tried askin' me a couple of times to leave. She'd even drawn up draft consent orders 'bout access with our son. She'd gotten help from one of 'er law lecturers.

'Not in a million years, bitch. If you think it was hard gettin' custody of Braydon, you've got no fuckin' idea… If you leave me, I will crucify you in Family Court. You'll be lucky to be gettin' supervised access once a year by the time I tell 'em all the dirt I got on ya. I can live with Mum in a house. Try sellin' this shit-box surrounded by junkie losers in Family Court, bitch. Besides, you're an ex-junkie, no judge in 'is right mind'll ever give ya custody over me. How long've ya been clean now? Two minutes?' She'd get all quiet then, have another drink, work 'erself up and then get lippy 'bout somethin' else. She didn't get that if she just shut her fucking mouth, it would all be over quicker.

Steve, the newspapers made out that I hit her over ev'ry little thing. It wasn't true. Sometimes, I let 'er get away with stuff, ya know. It's not like I hit *ev'ry* day. The papers made out I enjoyed floggun 'er. I didn't. It's not like I'm a psychopath or anythin'. I woulda loved to 'ave a girlfriend I never *needed* to lay a hand on.

*

Credit, where credit's due, mate, she never rang the cops *once* after we moved to those guvvy flats. She knew how close she come to losin' the kids before she went to the refuge when she was always ringin' the police on me, so she'd take the floggings, without callin' the cops. The neighbours were a different story.

One time, there was a loud knock on the door. I was in the middle of beltin' 'er. I'd thrown the phone at her nose and she was tryin' to stop the bleedin' with a buncha toilet paper. 'Get out of here!' she whispered real urgently. They knew I was hidin'. They were fucking pricks 'bout it too.

'What's this? *Law of Torts?*'

'I'm trying to finish my law degree,' she said softly.

'What happened to your nose?'

'It just started bleeding.'

'You must think we're stupid,' the cop said. His voice was hard and mean. 'Doing a law degree, hey? Not much point, is there?' The cop had a hint of Irish in 'is voice, 'You know he's not gunna stop until he kills you.' They found me on the roof. They locked me up for breach of bail. I wasn't supposed to go near 'er; let alone, throw phones at her nose. It was all right for them. They didn't 'ave a son to protect. I did.

*

Those fucking neighbours were a nightmare! Junkies and drunks, ev'ry one of them, but they'd hear 'er screamin' for me to stop or hear the thumpin' as I'd try 'n' snap her out of it and they'd call the cops. That July the cops came four or five times. I got locked up over and over for bashin' 'er, but the magistrate would let me out on bail the next mornin'. There was no jail in the city yet and the remand centre was pretty packed with 'ice' freaks.

The last time they bailed me to detox for a week. I caught the bus from detox straight back to her. I just kept goin' back for more of 'er abuse. I couldn't help meself.

She could get those scum bags to rally 'round 'er, somehow. She looked weak, I guess and I'm a pretty big bloke. She was tiny and her face covered in bruises could break ya heart. I went to get her from the club one Fridee night. She'd gone off with Crystal.

'What are ya doin'?' I asked her. I was fucking furious. She was at a club in the middle of the night, not drinkin', not gamblin'- who the fuck was she screwin'? When she answered, there was no hint of the poshness in her voice that pissed me off so much all the time. She sounded feral.

'Pete, I am getting away from you so that I can stay fucking sane!' She was a fucking lippy bitch, Steve. I clenched me teeth. I wasn't gunna hit her in front of all those people, but I balled me fists- so she knew what was comin'.

'You're comin' home right now!' I'll never forget it. Crystal egged them on, but a roomful of strangers in that pokey den started jeerin' at me. She looked at me, real defiant as she headed out the door to head home. There was no way in hell I was touchin' her face that night. Her kidneys were a different story.

Everyone in those flats hated me. By July, she hated me too. I knew it the day I got these fucking tatts. Look, I can handle a bitta pain, but it was fucking excruciatin' and Crystal was there, Willy was there, some other guys were there and she was there, too. I drank straight scotch or I wouldna survived. I was damned if I was gunna let them see me cry.

I was only gettin' the fucking things to put some money into their pockets, for fuck's sake, so they'd think 'bout it twice before ringin' the cops on me. They mighta hated me, but I knew me money was still good, when I came to score or get a backyard tattoo.

I asked for a Celtic 'V' for her on one arm and a Celtic 'M' for Michael on the other arm. It was painful, but I knew I hadda do it. Me eyes were waterin' by the end.

'You okay?' the prick kept askin', over 'n' over. The prick sounded like he was tryin' to hold back from laughin'. I looked at her at the end. She was beamin'. Watchin' me in pain had gotten the bitch off.

*

I never got really outta control when Michael was around, but if he was stayin' at Mum's, it was easy to just let rip, you know, Steve. I knew she'd never call the cops if me son wasn't around. She knew if I was in jail, Mum would just keep Michael 'till I was out. She woulda hadda go back to court to get 'im back 'n' she was terrified of that. Mum'd go for custody 'erself before givin' Michael back. She knew it. So, when Michael wasn't around, she took the beatings and she was quieter 'bout it.

*

On her birthday, she had just enough cash for a cask and she went out 'bout eight in the evenin' to buy it. Michael was down (for the night, we thought). Her last black eye was still healin' up and she was still walkun stiffly from the last poundin'.

'It's my birthday. I'm getting drunk tonight. You can do what you like to me tomorrow, Pete- just not tonight.' She wasn't hidin' her hatred anymore. She was holdin' out on givin' me sex more, too. Her voice was tired. She said it before she started drinkin'. She meant it.

You could just tell in the way she said things sometimes when she meant business.

Her tone made me nervous, mate. Somethin' bad was gunna happen. I could just feel it. So, I begged 'er to take it easy. 'Please, babe,' I said. She wouldn't listen. We had Michael with us that night, for fuck's sake! She wouldn't listen.

I knew as I struck 'er ribs I'd crossed the line. I was just tryin' to wake her up because Michael was cryin' and she was passed out on the sofa. I didn't mean to hit her so hard. We both heard the crack. She was pissed (drunk, not angry), but it was written all over 'er face. I tried to stop her leavin', but she got out. She made it outside to the phone box and dialled Triple 0.

Then, it was all 'bout damage control. I rang Andy to pick me up, told him she'd chucked Michael down the stairs. It felt good, with me brother backing me up, holding me son, before the police got there. She was at a neighbour's house, waitin' for the police to get there and we banged on the door until she opened it up. She kept the screen door locked. Andy, me brother, said to her, in his filthiest voice,

'You're never gonna see your son again, you psycho bitch.' She stood in the doorway, didn't look away, skulled a huge mug of wine defiant as and looked him in the eyes dead sober.

'We'll see about that.'

Letter 13

In Brief: Brent David Quarry, 33, has pleaded guilty to the murder of his ten-week old daughter on August 8, 2002. When Special Operations Group officers entered the flat in Melbourne, Quarry's de facto wife was unconscious and had sustained minor facial injuries. Brent David Quarry had a history of perpetrating domestic violence.

Dear Pete,

*T*he stories of the 'aha' moment are hard to listen to. After hearing so many of them, Pete, my ear is tuned to the unspoken and alert for the under-tones. Sometimes, there is disbelief (as in, 'Why did it take me so long to get it?'), there is often anger ('He told me he loved me!') and this may surprise you, but there is always grief.

I try to take time off work in July. Even the mere memory of that grief is hollowing.

Each time you touched me that winter, I flinched. It was reflexive by then, but it still enraged you. Do you know that I still know the lines on your palm like they are hard-wired into me? The memory of you raising your hand is so easy to bring to mind, even now, but I remember the feel of remorse in your finger-tips too and I think that loss pains me more than the memories of the beatings (I would never admit this to my clients, but in time, memories of so many assaults become indistinct from each other).

I struggle to remember the reasons for the beatings, these days, although, once upon a time, trying to fathom cause and effect, used to consume many sleepless hours. I remember that your accusations about imagined infidelities became more persistent, as autumn eased into winter.

Ironically, at the same time you were accusing me of sleeping 'with ev'ry man 'n' his dog', Crystal, who had been programmed for betrayal from the moment she was abused as a child, was persistently pestering me to join her on a promiscuous escapade. One afternoon, after shooting up amphetamines, Crystal found herself even more disin-bited than usual.

'There's a guy downstairs up for a threesome!' she said, bursting into my kitchen. I gave Crystal my standard answer,

'I'm too busy with the dishes.' She sighed, pouted and sat at my kitchen bench, obviously annoyed.

'Hon, if it's not too rude, can I ask why you're with him?' she asked in a petulant tone. 'It's not like he's faithful to you!' Crystal was the most audacious woman I have ever met. She said the words without a hint of irony. She had shamelessly seduced you and, yet, was not above raising the incident to suit her own agenda. And here's the thing... Crystal was so impossible to hate (or even stay angry at), in her total and utter brokenness, that the comment did not even cause a ripple in our conversation. I just gave her another one of my standard answers...

'He's Michael's Dad and he loves me.'

'Yeah, I know that, but, honey, you are gorgeous, do you know that?' I felt my face redden. I brushed off the compliment.

'Oh, come on!'

'Oh, stop with the fake modesty! It's me you're talking to.' We cackled. 'Seriously! You're beautiful and smart and, well, Lloydee- he's got that beard and that whole "I'm not very smart, but I can lift heavy things" thing happening.' I was laughing hysterically before she was even finished. Her rendition was priceless. When our laughter subsided, I finally faced her and thought about her question. I sighed.

'Crystal, the only way I know how to be, since I got clean, is to make a commitment and stick to it. Being a junkie was all about never sticking

to anything. Every day, I practice being different.' Looking back now, still trying to understand, I try to remember that lofty sense of commitment and find myself drawing a blank.

Perhaps, the truth was far less impressive. Maybe, I was primed for martyrdom from the moment I kicked my heroin habit and you saw that in me. Sobriety is, at its basest, dedication to self-denial (the air of hair-shirted redemption is always thick in those rooms where narcotics anonymous devotees meet). Perhaps, unthinking dedication to unconditional love just seemed like a more commendable cause than taking things 'one day at a time.'

I don't know, Pete... In all honesty, I may never find an answer to these uncomfortable questions. Whilst I have invested heavily in therapy so over-priced clinicians can tell me that resolution shouldn't bother me, sometimes I feel like the elusiveness of closure will drive me insane!

Although you probably won't believe me (God knows, you punished me repeatedly for enough imagined infidelities that winter!), the fact is that I never succumbed to the self-debasement of a threesome with Crystal. There was enough degradation in my life, so I did not look for more in meaningless sex.

And there was never another 'Gazza' moment, when I was caught off-guard, either, Pete. By then, I had lost my fondness for flirting. You had made every orgasm feel dirty for me, by that time. So, if the truth be told, I don't even remember desiring other men or being flattered by hints of male desire.

There was this as well, Pete... I think I stayed faithful because, in spite of everything, I still loved you. Maybe, it was just that simple.

Although I had tried so hard to rationalise a grand escape plan (I would finish my degree and leave you), I craved a different 'us' more strongly than I had ever ached for anything in my life (yes, Pete, even

181

heroin!). But I couldn't entertain denial forever and, eventually, even hope becomes too thread-bare to be useful.

After a while, I dreaded looking into those eyes I had once adored. Your eyes were so dark and hate-filled and the sadness left me sitting in the shower, one July morning, muffling sobs, as the hot water rained down on a body covered in the grey and purple marks of your contempt. Why was I so hard to love, Pete?

On my twenty-seventh birthday, I finally gave up. I dove into hastily skulled mugs of bad white wine and, when you raised your hand over my sleeping form and hit me hard enough to break a rib, I realised I had had enough (the aha! moment). You saw the decision in my eyes and I saw the response in yours. Let's not kid ourselves, Pete. You would have killed me, if I hadn't run.

With shrewdness that still impresses me, you developed an escape plan that was incredibly astute, Pete. You and your brother grabbed Michael and drove away. I was making a statement to a police officer, who was mentally contemplating the headaches of interstate extradition, by the time you and your brother had crossed the border. Touche, Pete!

For a while, the need to ring you in the remand centre was compulsive. Crystal dragged me to the pub, sensing my need for respite. I drank quickly, reaching for the reprieve of intoxication, which seemed to stubbornly elude me. That night, a fat man, with wise eyes, approached me, as he was leaving the pub, and handed me a business card. He leaned down to whisper in my ear,

'I have two spare rooms. Call me when you're ready to leave him.'

One day, I dared to defy the insistent compulsions of the patterns-painful, though familiar- that had governed my life. I didn't ring you in remand that day. I rang Russ instead.

V

She didn't make a clean break right away. I hadda turn meself into the cops in the city. Until I crossed the state border, I was untouchable without an extradition warrant. No one could be bothered with interstate extradition over a crummy breach of bail charge in a domestic violence matter so I stayed at Mum's for a bit, worked meself up to crossin' the border.

When I rang her she was furious,

'What did you tell them?'

'Don't make me say it.' I was cryin' because I knew she expected me to be cryin'. I felt a bit bad about what I'd done, but she hadda know she pushed me to it.

'Tell me *now* what you told the police and why they won't bring me my son back from your mother's place,' she said. Her voice was so firm, filthy and hard. I started bawlin'.

'Please don't do this babe.'

'Tell me now or I'm hanging up.' She could be so hard, sometimes, Steve.

'I told them you threw him down the stairs and that's why I hit you.'

'You are a fucking arsehole! Honestly! How do you live with yourself, Pete?' The coldness in 'er voice was like a knife through me.

'Please, I've gotta hand meself into the cops. I'm scared, babe. I need you.' I was cryin' hard now. I knew she wouldn't resist.

She caught the bus over the border to see me. Like I said, Steve, she was always there for me when I needed 'er. I booked a motel room. I made love to her in the spa. She was frantic, when she came. I went down on her for the first time ever and she came again. I knew it might be the last time for a while so I wanted her to remember...

She caught the bus with me to the cops in the city, where I was goin' to turn meself in. She was walkun a bit stiffly 'coz of the rib I'd broken on her birthday and 'coz I'd just fucked her brains out. I put me arm 'round her on the bus, careful to stay away from 'er ribs.

'You'll wait for me, right?' I asked nervously.

'Of course, I will. You'll be fine,' she said. She was so blasé. A part of 'er'd already moved on. I could see it in 'er eyes. She wanted 'er son back. That was why she was 'ere; pumping me for info so she could work out 'er strategy for court. She was a fucking whore, mate. She was as bad as Crystal, when it came to fucking someone to get what she wanted- only smarter and colder.

She didn't give a shit about me anymore and it killed me to see it. But I pretended to meself. I hadda, mate. When I walked into the police station, knowin' they were gunna lock me up, I didn't care 'bout any of it. I handled all of the shit I knew they were gunna put me through 'coz I kept kiddin' meself she was gunna be there on the other end.

I was in remand when she stopped callin' to see how I was doin'. I still held out hope. When me bail appeal worked, about a month later, I booked a motel room, again, I left a message for her, I waited for her. She never came.

In an affidavit, later, she reckoned I'd left thirty-two messages on her phone that night. They got more 'n' more abusive. At first, I was pissed at her for not turnin' up. Later, I was threatenin' to come 'n' get her 'n' bash up anyone who got in me way.

She started comin' to Family Court with a guy- some big fat dude... one of Crystal's ex-fucks, no doubt. I'm no oil painting, but I could not see what she saw in 'im.

It was no holds barred after that. I threw ev'ry accusation I could at her.

She was hooked on smack. She was a speed freak. She was crazy 'coz of post-natal depression. Anything I could accuse her of I did.

While the bitch scrambled 'round disproving the accusations, the judge wouldn't give her sole custody of me son. She hadda share custody with me mother and she hated that.

But what could she do? She was on record admittin' she was a heroin addict. That's how she got on the methadone programme, in the first place. She'd conned that letter outta her doctor about the post-natal depression to try 'n' keep me outta jail. I had the upper hand and you'd better believe I was gunna use it.

She walked past me in reception of the Federal Court building one time, while we were waitin' for our case to get called and I whispered, 'I still love you.' She was too far gone. She wouldn't even look at me.

The bitch was fucking smart. She pulled out the weekly urine tests from when she had gone off the methadone programme, before she got pregnant with Michael. She stopped me usin' me lawyer, 'coz she'd gotten legal advice from him on the receivin' stolen goods thing. She went and got psych exams that proved she wasn't crazy. She started bringin' in brand new urine tests to prove she wasn't takin' speed.

It's not hard. You can get a clean urine after two days with speed! It takes months with weed. She had the upper hand now and she was usin' it. Fucking bitch!

inside_Updated.indd 185 3/31/2012 7:24:35 PM

I was standin' in court unrepresented by the time we went to the hearin' in Family Court- all because of her. Do you know the crazy thing, Steve? I think I coulda handled all of it, except her face. She hated me, man. It fuckin' drove me to tears, as I talked to the judge.

'What about her abuse?' I asked desperate. Her face was so cold, so filled with hate. I'd been inside this chick, watched her face, as she came. The contrast was fucking too much to take!

In the end, it took her over a year, but by the time she was finished, I couldn't see me son unless me Mother was supervisin' me. The fat dude saw more of Michael 'n' was more of a father to 'im than I was.

In the end, mate, I couldn't help, but remember 'er face, skullin' wine and facin' off with Andy. She'd known what she was gunna do back then, in that moment. Just like she'd known how she was gunna use Crystal the first time she saw her. Like I said, mate, she was the fucking smartest, coldest bitch I've ever met.

She'd finished 'er law degree, by the time she'd finished screwun me in court. When she went into practice, she specialised in workin' with battered women. That was what Mum said. That's what they said in the papers too. I never thought she'd make it through 'er degree. I shoulda known. She'd used ev'ry bit of legal knowledge she had to screw me, in Family Court.

And you know, what, Steve? I still loved her. I woulda taken her back in a heartbeat.

Letter 14

Local News, 3 March 2003

A twenty-two year old police officer, Felicity Park, has been found dead in her burnt-out home in the Perth suburb, Hilarys. Her partner has been charged with assault, pending the post-mortem investigation. Police Commissioner Matthews made a statement today, in which he said, 'No one is immune from the possibility of domestic violence.'

Dear Pete,

*I*n a rare comment about all of it, a while ago, my husband told me, with the most sorrowful eyes,

'I just wish you never thought about it; that what happened didn't enter your mind.'

I can appreciate the sentiment. In the early days, every bearded stranger walking past could evoke a racing heart and a dry mouth. Sometimes, walking in the city, I still have to stop, find an alley, where I can discreetly crumble so I can hold my head between my legs and get the blood running back to my brain again.

I wish that I didn't have to stifle that uneasy feeling of being smothered each time my sons cuddle me just a little too hard for just a little too long. The need to hold them a little at arms' length is there, even now, after all the hurt and the fear of losing them is long gone.

And every year, when I pack away the boxes of photographs, affidavits, police statements and other hoarded tokens, I try to do it with grace. Sometimes, I can muster gratitude for the motley crew of junkies, alcoholics, sluts and ex-cons with land-lines, who saved my life by dialling Triple 0 and an obese, altruistic stranger, who gave me a place to stay and expected nothing in return. Some years, I am even thankful to the disgruntled, burnt-out police officers, tired of coming, who came anyway.

But, Pete, here's the thing… every year it takes thirty-one days to.process the grief and guilt and to burst that hard ball of bitterness in the pit of my stomach. At the end of all of it, the rage is so close

to simmering to a boil that it could overwhelm everything; my anger is awesome enough to overpower the fragile membrane of normality that I cultivate with so much care. Big enough to disseminate the good suits, the glasses of fine, red wine, the birthday parties, the soccer games, the sandwiches without crusts, the diligence and gentle intimacy of a good marriage and everything else in its wake.

Why, Pete? The question is a furious scream and an exhausted whisper, both at once.

And the longing for the life I was meant to have sometimes feels like it might erupt through my clenched fists, my tightened jaw and my 'all cried out' eyes. These days, I use it (all of it) and I am renowned for being a 'hard-as-nails' advocate in court rooms. I stare down men (more fearsome than you) for a living now, Pete.

I try not to lose. But there are defeats. And they always feel like the punches you used to aim at my lower back; the ones that seemed to make my kidneys rattle.

The victories aren't much better. Sometimes, when I'm in court and the magistrate reaches the decision I was after or a favourable out-of-court settlement is reached, I turn to my client. Shell-shocked, there is always an astonished expression in her eyes. I see the familiar question clearly, 'What now?'

All of it – my three-year-old son standing in a washing basket in the cold, a broken rib on my birthday, the perpetually bruised eyes, the persistent, niggling taunts meant to erode me, the forceful blow-jobs to prove a point, pressing your thumbs hard into my larynx to assert your authority, the fucking through blood– all of it... has no meaning. Longing to extinguish the question year after year, I am furious at myself, at you, at a God I no longer believe in, because closure is just another myth.

In August, as my birthday draws closer, I cannot help but remember my birthday statement to that police officer, when I realised I had finally had enough. Although my memory of making that statement is a little hazy, I vividly remember that the police officer asked me to go back a couple of days in my narrative. I started recounting events in a voice that was perpetually flat by then and she interrupted me,

'So you had sex with him after he did that to you?' I remember feeling stunned that she required an explanation.

'Yes,' I said softly, a little confused.

'Why did you do that?' I was dumb-struck. In my world, there were no reasons anymore. You didn't need to have a reason for having sex with a man, who had just abused you. You just did it. In that moment, I was lost for words. Not much has changed, Pete.

So, I find comfort where I can. Little things matter.

These days, I keep my favourite photograph of myself in my post-Pete life on my new mantlepiece. The photo is only a few years old. My husband and my sons came to watch my graduation ceremony. After I'd politely shaken the dean's hand and accepted my diploma, I started walking away and the boys whooped loudly and inappropriately. 'Go Mum!' Braydon cheered. Using a zoom lens, my husband caught my expression in that moment. I am smiling a little awkwardly, my face is lined, but there is hope in my eyes again. And most days I can tell myself (and believe it when I think it), that maybe this was the life I was meant to live, after all.

V

*

I went into drug rehab in March, when Michael wasn't even two, remember? I was sick of meself, the pot and the booze. It was only about seven months into the no holds barred, fucking Family Court war. She'd brung over twenty clean urines to court by then (some old, some new). I hadn't come up with one, yet.

I asked 'er to come visit me in rehab one weekend and she did. I made out I wanted to make peace with 'er so we could sort the Michael stuff out without having to drag it through court.

When she got there, I came clean about why I asked her to come.

'I want you back. That's why I'm gettin' clean. Tell me there's a chance.' She looked so uncomfortable, she played with 'er hands, she looked away. Then she took a deep breath and looked me in the eye.

'You need to focus on yourself, right now,' she said 'n' 'er eyes were desperate, 'I want you to get well for Michael.'

'What do you see in that fat dude? Is it because he's rich and he's got a job? Because I'll do that, ya know.' She laughed.

'He's not rich and he's not my lover, Pete.' I felt hope for a second, but then 'er face lit up. I hated that her face lit up like that, when she talked 'bout him. 'But he *is* my best friend, Pete, and that's what I need right now- a friend. He makes me laugh. He makes me think and I like who I am when I'm with him.'

'And us?' She smiled. She still remembered. First she tried being real glib, you know,

'I'm a great lay, Pete, I know, but you can do better!' she said. She laughed to break the tension. Then her face got serious. When she started talkun again, her voice was so gentle, so sweet that I coulda cried. 'We weren't right for each other, you know that. So, stay in here and get well -for Michael- if you can't do it for yourself. Just hang in there, please.' I couldn't stand it. I wanted her back so badly. I could feel me chance slippin' away, through me fingers.

'I never told ya this,' I said real slow, bitin' my lip, concentratin' real hard on not bawlin', 'but I'd had one-night stands before you. You were me first real relationship. I know I messed up, but you are the first chick I've ever been in love with.' She looked at me squarely. She spoke so gently and calmly,

'When Richard left me, it devastated me. That's half the reason I was so messed up, when I met you, Pete. He was my first love. I know what it feels like to lose the first person you've ever loved, but you've got to believe me, it *will* get better.' She squeezed me hand and I dropped the subject.

We talked for hours. She told me 'bout bein' diagnosed with P.T.S.D.

'It terrified me that it was going to come out in court, you know, but I'm so glad I kept on going to the psychologist. I've learnt not to be afraid of everything anymore.' I held her hand in mine. She was lookin' at the ground.

'Are you okay?'

'I'm fine,' she said. She looked me in the eye; her chin held up high, but her eyes were misty. 'Russ has been really supportive, too.'

I hugged her when she left. She'd been such a skank and she'd turned her life around. Part of me was kinda jealous, but bein' 'round her made me think I could do this- or anythin', for that matter. Fuck, I'd missed her!

And you know what, mate? I seen this in her, the first time I met her, man. I seen the fact that she could do anythin' she put 'er mind to the first time I met 'er. It had scared the fuck outta me then. Now, I loved 'er for it.

She started answerin' me calls twice a week when I'd ring to talk to Michael. I felt like I was gettin' her on side. Somethin' else started to happen. I saw her- maybe for the first time.

She wasn't just sexy. She was sweet 'n' smart. I never ever really seen 'er before, Steve, 'coz of the pot and the booze and all the other stuff that was goin' on. She cared 'bout me- if only 'coz I was the father of her child. She'd spend an hour on the phone, when I was havin' a bad day in rehab. Yeah, she'd been crazy, when we been together, but she'd had so much on her plate, mate.

Think about it. In just one fucking year, she got off the 'done and got custody of 'er son, she gave birth to me son, she moved house (twice, mind you, 'coz she hadda get away from me after the thing with Braydon, remember?), she finished her Arts degree and went back to finish her law degree. I know she was a bit of a manic, psycho, stuck-up bitch to start with, but how could ya not go a little bit crazy with that much shit goin' on?

All the while, she stayed off smack and she went without stuff so she could buy me weed. And, mate, think 'bout where we were livin'! How fucking easy would it have been for her to just go back on the gear? There was a smack dealer livin' at the end of 'er block o' flats, for fuck's sake! In rehab, I finally saw how hard it musta been for 'er to stay clean.

For the first time, I really didn't want to lose her. Not just 'coz of the sex, but because I finally appreciated 'er. I *liked* her for the first time

194

when I realised how awesome the chick was. It's like I said, mate, she was always there for me.

Steve, I know you don't see it, but, mate, you never lived with 'er. You hated her on sight so you never spent much time with 'er. Honestly, mate, I still feel stupid I missed it, man.

Sometimes it was hard. Rehab was no fucking picnic, let me tell ya.

'I love you,' I told 'er one night on the phone. I'd had a shitty day in rehab. Rehab's full of fuckers into head games, man. I was mean to 'er, I know. 'Stop pissin' in me pocket and tell me if there's a chance.' She was quiet for a long time. She was cryin', when she answered,

'I want you to get well.'

'It's all right for you… you've moved on, you've got a brand new life!' I sounded petty, I know.

'Please don't do this,' she begged me, 'I'm trying to be here for you… I can't do it, if you do this.'

'I'm sorry,' I said. I didn't want her to hang up. 'I've had a shit of a day.'

'Me too,' she said. She started laughin'. I started laughin', too. 'Here's a thought. You tell me about your shitty day and I'll tell you about mine.'

And that's what we did, from then on, two times a week, like clock-work. Tellin' her the details of my fuckin' schedule, tellin' her 'bout somethin' funny thing that happened at an Narcotics Anonymous meetin' or about some head-fucking moron, who was pushin' me buttons that day- it made it better.

She'd tell me 'bout the kids or some drop-kick at work (She was finishun her internship, by then, I think). Sometimes, she sounded

195

so tired, but she'd listen to me for ages 'till I was done. I dunno what it was about her voice over that phone line. I only know she got me through me stint in rehab just by makin' the time to do somethin' so simple. She listened to me talkun on the phone twice a week.

Other times, she talked 'bout Michael's day or the latest thing our son was doin'.

'He has the worst taste in music, Pete. Hip hop settles him when he can't sleep!' I realised in rehab, mate, that she couldna fallen in love with our son with everythun that was goin' on in the first year of his life. I understood that now. I shouldna been so hard on 'er.

I fell in love with her, Steve, just talkun to her on the phone. I'd be lyin' if I said *all over again*. I fell in love with her for the first time. I was hooked on the sex before. Now, I wanted to spend the rest of me life with this smart, sexy, funny chick.

Then it happened. She called. I was still in rehab. We still hadn't got the final orders in Family Court and Mum'd decided she was gunna try and get custody of Michael so Mum was always tryin' to dig up dirt on her. I can't believe I was so fucking stupid, man. I shoulda known better. We both know what Mum's like 'bout her grand-kiddies.

It was weird for me to get a call from her. I was always the one that called 'er. I always rang on the days and times written in our interim Family Court orders. I chatted to Michael for two secs, before askin' 'im to give 'is Mum the phone. It was weird, her callin' me. I knew somethin' was off. She sounded furious.

'I've got this letter in front of me.'

'Yeah! And?'

'Your mother's lawyer understands I've been diagnosed with a psychiatric disorder. She wonders what the details of this are, because she's concerned for her grandson's safety.' Fuck! I'd been tryin' to convince Mum how much she'd changed. I'd told her about the P.T.S.D.

Fuck, fuck, fuck!

Me mind was racin'. I hadda fix this or I was gunna lose her, once and for all.

'I didn't tell her,' I lied. I said the first thing that popped into me head, 'It musta been your lawyer.' I started bawlin', if you can picture it, mate. Holdin' this pay phone in me hand in rehab fuckin' bawlin' me eyes out, but I just couldn't fuckin' believe Mum had screwed it all up. I was beggin' her, for fuck's sake, when I said, 'Please, please believe me.' She sighed.

'Okay.'

'Thank you! Thank you! Please don't give up on me,' I begged. Me voice was desperate. I was beggin' her, mate! I was in fucking tears! In the end, I think I was cryin' from relief. I thought I'd pulled it off.

I hadn't. She didn't believe me lies. She never rang me again. She never spoke to me on the phone again for the rest of 'er life.

I've had a lotta time to think 'bout why. It was one more of 'er fucking mind-games. She'd told me 'bout the P.T.S.D to test me. Just like with the Crystal thing. The freaky bitch could just never take me word on anythin'. What kind of relationship is that, when you can't trust the person you're supposed to spend the rest of ya life with so you test them over and over 'bout ev'ry little thing?

*

I tried everythin'. I tried askin' Michael to give 'er the phone, when I rang 'im. She wouldn't take it. One time I tied up her line for hours from a pay-phone. She still didn't talk to me.

I tried leavin' abusive messages on her phone to try 'n' stir 'er up and make 'er pick up. She reported them to the police, without ever sayin' a word to me.

I sent her texts. That was fucking suicidal! There were a coupla text messages they pulled out for me trial, where I called her a 'slut'. They were a coupla years old. She must have saved ev'ry abusive message and text I ever sent to her, over the years. Like I said, Steve, the bitch was cold.

I couldn't do it anymore. I left rehab. If she wasn't gunna be there on the other end, there was no point.

*

I found 'er. Remember that time I borrowed your car? The time I said I hadda go to a job interview? Well, I used ya car to follow 'er after she picked Michael up from Mum's.

I watched 'er house for weeks. I moved into a crappy bed-sitter 'round the corner. Her house was beautiful. I tried the doors, when I knew that everyone was outta the house. It was months before I finally got in. One night the door was unlocked. I walked through the house, I smelt me son's clothes, I felt 'er panties and I almost lost it.

I knew I couldn't let her know I been there so I put everythin' back. I stopped meself from takin' a dump in the fat-fuck's shoes in the cupboard.

Sometimes, I followed her on the bus. She'd drop Braydon off to school and walk Michael across the road to day-care, then she'd

198

catch the bus to her fancy job in the city. It was a crowded bus and I'd sit up the back with me cap sittin' low over me face. Sometimes, I'd follow when she got off the bus in the city. Not often. I stood out like a sore thumb 'round all those office workers. I couldn't risk her seein' me.

I knew I couldn't let her see me, but I'd sneak long hard looks at her. She looked exhausted still. Her life was still just a buncha errands 'n' chores. So, why couldn't she be with me?

She got 'arder to follow after she bought the car, but, sometimes I'd just stand in the bushes in 'er yard at night, smoking and hopin' to get a glimpse of her naked. I never did, but I'd stare for hours at 'er face, while she sat watchin' TV or muckin' around on 'er laptop. She'd look 'round all the time, stare out the window and I'd hide me ciggie so she couldn't see the flame. She looked so paranoid 'n' scared.

Then, just like that, she was gone! Her place was up for rent. I hung 'round at Michael's day-care centre and at Braydon's school at the bus stop, but she was gone. Little Michael started talkun, when 'e came for access visits. He talked about long bus trips, but 'e was too young to make sense. I didn't know where they were, but it sounded far 'way.

I tried waitin' 'round at bus interchanges. It was fucking hopeless. She was gone.

I coulda found her again, if I'd kept on tryin', but I was tired, Steve. If she wanted to get away from me that badly, maybe, I just hadda let her go. The final orders come through by then and I'd been screwed. She 'n' Mum had ganged up on me so I could only see Michael in the school holidays if Mum supervised me. Plus, I wasn't allowed to be 'round at hand-overs.

For years, she wouldn't take me calls. When I worked out where she was, it was 'coz Michael had learnt to talk. I couldn't afford the bus fare to keep watchin' 'er. I stopped ringin' Michael after a while. What was the point? I moved to Queensland to start over.

There were other chicks in between. It was never the same. It was like smoking pot, when you were hanging out for a heroin or speed rush, or smoking the leaf, when you really needed a stick of good, solid heads of weed... she ruined me for anyone else.

Ev'ry relationship I was in failed *because of her*. I only wanted one woman and she hated me so much she didn't wanna ever speak to me again. The bitch knew how to make a statement. She organised her life 'round never havin' to see me or speak to me again for the rest of 'er life.

Letter 15

Local News, 13th August 2009

Bowan Wade, 19 has been charged with the murder of his ex-girlfriend, Clarissa Callow, 17. The two had arranged to meet at a storage shed in Stanthorpe on Sunday afternoon so Clarissa could retrieve her belongings. The relationship had broken up two weeks before and Clarissa complained to friends that Wade was stalking her. Police discovered Clarissa's body in the storage shed on Monday, August 10, 2009 at approximately 4pm. Police allege that the couple began arguing, before Wade killed her and left her lifeless body in the storage shed.

Dear Pete,

*I*t is already August and tomorrow I turn thirty-four. Although August is always a hard month for me, this year doesn't feel so bad. So, maybe, writing these letters has been helpful after all, even if I will never send them to anyone.

I'm standing on the deck, looking out at the ocean with my first cigarette of the day. Every week day, I let go of half my work-day on the twenty-minute drive home on the highway. With a cigarette and a swig of beer, I let go of the rest.

Sometimes, my husband joins me on the deck. We have a routine.

'Those things will kill you,' he will say. On cue, I quip,

'Everything fun is lethal.'

'Saved any lives today?' he will ask.

'No, too busy with Legal Aid claims. What about you? Hacked into the World Bank yet?'

'Nah, too busy with programming code.'

We composed this routine years ago, when we realised we could not talk civilly about work with each other. He no more understands me choosing a career that exposes me to trauma than I understand why he is paid obscene amounts of money to sit at home in his track-suit pants playing with computer programming code.

When the routine's complete, we kiss deeply and passionately. On some days, when he holds me, when that swig of beer hasn't quite

washed away the remnants of my day, I close my eyes and remember-
the boys, a life we've built together and an ocean in walking distance
that still holds the power to soothe my soul.

In his forties, greying at the temples, almost morbidly obese, Russ still gets
a kick out of holding my hand. I like that about him. I like that he leaves
the demons alone, doesn't need to ask why I need to walk to the beach at
two a.m., sometimes, just to feel the wet sand on the soles of my feet.

For Russ, it has always been enough to live in the here and now and not
think too much about it. We pay our bills, raise our kids, make love, eat
good food, occasionally get drunk on good wine, work at jobs we enjoy
and live somewhere beautiful. What more is there to think about? Some
days, I feel so envious I want to throttle him. Most days, I can summon
gratitude I found him in an inner-city pub all those years ago.

Russ always says he knew he was going to marry me the first time he
saw me in that inner-city pub. He'd never seen anyone skull a schooner
of beer so fast.

'I knew you'd be fun.'

For my part, I was far less certain. I wasn't ever going to let myself fall
in love again.

Years ago, I panicked. That was the first time I got the urge to run.

It was just after our matter was mentioned in court, Pete. I had just
finished listening to a Family Court judge consider the very lawyerly
argument that, notwithstanding the fact that you had been convicted
of a domestic violence offence, my tolerance of your violence could be
indicative of serious mental health issues.

Standing outside the Federal Court building defiantly inhaling a cigarette, while I watched your ultra-Christian mother across the road
conversing jovially with her solicitor (the author of the very lawyerly

argument that had left me reeling), I felt something inside me deflate. I welcomed the thought of giving up, in that moment, wondering if I had any reserves left to keep on fighting.

And, of course, it was July... That day, Braydon was with his dad- so it must have been a Monday. I packed everything I treasured into that pale blue Datsun Sunny Boy I drove at the time (I'd christened her "Bertha"). I donated the rest of my things to St. Vincent de Paul, left my keys to Russ' place in his letter box and I just started driving.

When the dry grass of drought-affected plains gave way to the lush greenery on the highway, I stopped holding my breath. Winding down the tight corners of the mountain, heading for the coast, I felt free.

I never did ask him how he found me, but a few days later, I was standing in a queue at the check-out counter of a supermarket in a coastal country town with a population of just on five thousand people. I didn't know the curves of his mighty back as well as I do now and I guess I was distracted, but when he asked for a soft pack of Stuyvesant Filters, I recognised his voice. He didn't smoke, but I did and, in those days, that was my brand. When he turned around and handed me the pack of cigarettes, he said softly,

'V, it's time to come home. Michael's coming tomorrow.'

Russ and I have never talked about that day. We drove the four hours back to his place in silence. I like that about him too.

We have made a life near the beach. When the anxiety hits, standing in the dark, my bare feet on wet sand, eyes closed, listening to the waves still calms me, even now, years later. If I focus on breathing, the urgent need to run slowly abates.

He loves me. He loves the boys. He is a good man. You will never understand this, Pete, but it is enough to hang a life on.

V

*

When she texted me, it was years since I'd talked to 'er. 'We need to talk about Michael,' she wrote in 'er text. 'I'm in Queensland,' I texted back. 'I'll come to you. Whereabouts in Queensland r you?' she texted me back. I waited for ages, before replyin'. I wish, to God, I never replied at all, but, like I said, Steve, it was always like that with us; we couldn't stay away from each other.

Finally, I sent her a text, tellin' 'er where I was livin'. She texted back the name of the motel where she'd be stayin' and a time for me to come over. I dressed careful. I was nervous as hell when I knocked on the door. I didn't know how I was gunna feel when I saw her.

It was right at the end o' November and it was fuckin' hot, so she was dressed simple. She had a long black dress on and a thick leather belt. Her hair was tied back with a shiny silver scarf thing. Mum'd told me she wore glasses now so I was not surprised that she had these nerdy, glasses on with chunky silver frames. I'll give her this. Her sense of style had improved. She didn't look like a slut anymore.

'What's this about?' I asked. I was scared shitless, but I wanted the upper hand at the start and I hadda let her know that. So, I tried to sound mean and pissy with 'er. Deep down, I was pretty prepared to accept that I hadda take anythin' she was gunna do to me, but, Steve, what more could she take from me?

'I'm dying.' She looked me straight in the eye. Her voice was matter of fact.

'Bull shit!' It was another one of her head-games. She didn't skip a beat, passed me a piece of paper. The letters blurred, but I picked up the gist: 'inoperable tumour', 'terminal', 'twelve months', 'palliative care.' Me chest tightened. I had no idea what she expected of me. I said what I think she wanted to hear.

'I'm sorry.'

'Don't be sorry.' She was beaming when she said it. She smiled and her voice was firm, but light. She still talked posh, but she didn't sound like she was tryin' to lord it over you anymore. 'We are going to make love one *last* time. We are going to drink a beer together for the *last* time and we are going to talk about our son's future like adults... I don't have a lot of time. I need us to do this.' Her eyes were begging me. I can be a prick, but I felt so bad for her.

What was I supposed to say, Steve? What d'ya say to a chick, who took everythin' from ya, who you think about constantly, when she says she's gunna fuck ya, one last time, before she dies? I tried to be staunch, ya know.

'You think I'm gunna fuck you after everythun you done to me?' I asked. My stomach was churnin'. I was angry and sad and me head was spinning. This was too weird and too much.

She slipped off her belt. She slipped her dress off. She stood there in black lace knickers and a black lace bra. She looked me in the eye. No hesitation. No 'victim' thing happenin' anymore. She was so fucking strong and sexy and confident.

'Yes, I do.'

And I did. I couldn't help meself. I wanted to be strong enough to walk out the door or to say, 'Fuck you!', but, there she was, undressed and sexy and strong. I wanted her, man.

She was a bit thicker 'round 'er middle. Her tits were saggier now, but she was still the most amazun fuck. We made love and it was so fucking hot. I wanted her so badly. I bit her nipples, thrust inside her hard. 'Harder!' she whispered firmly. I didn't want it to end, so I kept pullin' out of 'er to pace meself.

At one point she cried and trembled, 'I don't want to die, Pete.' I held her and eased her tears away with me tongue. When we came, finally, we came at the same time and it was even better than the old days. She was outta breath and beautiful.

'Fuck!' She smiled as she said it. She collapsed on me chest, spent, her love juices oozing down 'er thighs. She kissed me chest softly. 'Fuck!' she said again and shook her head. Her face at that moment haunts me, Steve. She was so incredibly fucking beautiful.

'Yeah, if this is all we ever did, we coulda lasted, I reckon,' I said it casual and laughed, but bein' inside her again'd devastated me. I looked at her lyin' on me chest and I knew what I'd lost. What was wrong with me Steve? Why didn't I deserve to have this?

'As I recall,' she started, in her posh voice, 'this was almost all we ever did.' She laughed then and shook her head, rememberin'. She slipped on a robe and asked if I wanted a beer.

She returned with two glasses filled with beer.

'To new beginnings and happy endings!' she said, holding up her glass in a kind of weird toast. Fuck me! What the fuck was she going on about? She blew it with those words! I remembered why it had never worked out between us. The fucking bitch was crazy still.

'Whatever.' We touched our glasses and skulled our beers. Gulpin' 'n' burpin', we looked at each other and laughed. When we laughed together, in that moment, it was like the old days- the good bits of the old days- like that time I'd taken 'er out to dinner 'n' she'd worn that sexy, black dress 'n' she only had eyes for me- when I was proud as punch that this chick was mine for keeps.

The next thing I remember I was on the bed. For some reason, there was blood everywhere, Steve.

It took me a second to remember where I was. I gagged when I saw 'er. Her neck was sliced in two. Her face was all bloody. She was all hacked up between 'er legs. There was a knife stickin' outta her stomach. I couldn't remember a thing. I couldn't think how I coulda done this.

I shoulda rung the police there and then. I didn't. I just got dressed quick smart and fumbled for the door, got outta there and just went 'ome. I didn't even wipe down doors and walls or anythin'. Steve, I wasn't tryin' to escape anythin' I done. I just ran from shock. I just wanted to get away from the sight of 'er.

They said later that made me look guilty. Me girlfriend, Gab, was goin' off her brain, when the cops came to pick me up and they hand-cuffed me.

'Leave him alone, you pigs!' she screamed, her kid restin' on 'er hip. I was shell-shocked, mate. I couldn't say a thing.

They didn't believe she drugged me. When the test came back positive for the methadone, they reckoned I'd used it to get the courage up to do what I done to 'er.

Gab bailed out, when I came clean that I'd fucked her.

'You always told me how crazy she was. How could you be so stupid? You know she always got off on pushin' your buttons. Now look at you.' She looked at me with disgust and I never saw her again.

Steve, I couldn't understand it. I still can't. I loved her. I coulda never done that to her. They said the vaginal hacking and the letters 'slut' carved into 'er face showed a personal connection between her and 'er killer. Me semen was inside her. That didn't help. They found a syringe; traces of heroin, her blood, and me finger-prints on it. That didn't help either.

But I swear to you, man, I dunno how that happened! I wouldn't know where to start scorin' heroin, these days, you gotta believe me!

They found me prints on the knife, the texts on her phone. The clincher was a contract a solicitor had drawn up for me to sign- transferrin' me parental rights to Russ- the fat dude. They reckoned I'd been so outraged by her suggestion I'd killed her.

I tried to convince me lawyer I was bein' framed. I told him about the tumour. He didn't believe she hadn't talked 'bout parental rights with me. Her text made it seem like that's what she'd wanted to do all along. He didn't believe she'd thrown 'erself at me to fuck 'er. 'Your best bet is to plead guilty, mate.' I couldn't do it. I couldn't go to jail. I'd spent a month in remand for breachin' bail years ago. I wasn't goin' back.

*

Maybe, I shoulda followed his advice. The evidence was fucking brutal. Some doctor testified she had at least twelve months to live, that she'd started accessin' a support group for the terminally ill.

Russ- the fat dude- testified how much she hated me guts. He was not teary in court. He was a hard-ass. His eyes were fucking murderous and he looked at me with a 'fuck you' expression.

'My *wife* never would have voluntarily had sex with him. She hated him.' He stressed the word *wife* just to rub me nose in it.

The fat dude requested permission from the court for him and Braydon, her son, to make victim impact statements. In his victim impact statement, he said,

'The worst thing about what he did was that my wife hadn't even told me she was dying yet. We'd survived so much together. We survived a long battle through Family Court with *him*.' He spat the word 'him' out with such disgust that I knew she'd spun her sad-ass, 'victim' stories for him.

210

'We survived her finishing her degree and then working hard in the field and having no time for anything. We would have worked through this. I didn't get the chance to help her die in peace. After seven years, devoting myself to this woman and her children- as her friend, at first and later, as her husband- I wanted the opportunity to *try*, at least, to make it okay for her. He robbed me of that.' He paused and cleared his throat. When he started talkun again, he could barely contain his anger,

'I also hate what he did to my wife's legacy. She spent the last years of her life devoted to helping women escaping domestic violence and, in the end, she couldn't protect herself. That's the sound-bite he turned her life into and he should be punished severely for that.' He looked at me then. The fat dude woulda killed me if we weren't in a court room. I knew it.

Braydon musta been thirteen or fourteen by the time I was up for sent'ncin' and he was still posh and still ferret-faced and dweeby. He had a tie on and a dress shirt and he had a bit of a tummy on 'im. Not like me Michael, who was always rake thin. When he read the statement, he stopped 'n' started a bit, but he was very moving to listen to. Just like 'is Mother.

'I don't remember what Pete did to me when I was little. I only know my Mother was guilty and ashamed that she hadn't protected me. When she asked me if I remembered, her face was very sad.' He took a breath and read on, 'She worked with lots of women, who'd been through domestic violence because she thought she could help some women and children to avoid what we'd been through.' He paused, cleared his throat and read on, 'My Mum lived a very stressful life. She studied and worked very hard and worried about the people she helped and worried about me and my brother. Sometimes, she was so tired, she'd fall asleep, when I needed help with my homework. I didn't like her for that.'

Fuck me dead! Even my heart was breakin' as he finished, Steve! The honesty was just too fucking much! He didn't really look like her, but he sounded so much like her, you know. I looked straight ahead, focused on a bit of brown panelling. I remembered me lawyer's advice not to cry.

'But my Mother was there at awards nights and soccer games and she arranged the *best* sleep-overs for me and my friends. She'd take us to the beach even though she hated swimming and she saved up to buy us cool presents at Christmas and on our birthdays. She didn't deserve to die.' He didn't look at me. The fat dude had tears in his eyes and squeezed Braydon's shoulder, when Braydon walked back to sit next to him.

I guess the sentence shouldna surprised me. The chick was a lawyer, for fuck's sake! For the judge and all the other fucking lawyers in that court-room (even mine, probably), it was personal. Like I said before, Steve, she was one of theirs. Plus, the facts were 'gainst me. A woman can't commit suicide by slashin' 'er own throat, carvin' the word 'slut' into 'er face and hackin' up 'er own vagina.

But somehow she did, Steve! I know it sounds crazy, but she did this to 'erself and to me!

Maybe she drove me to it and I don't remember, but I doubt it, mate. Steve, I just can't imagine meself doin' somethin' so horrific to the mother of me child. Why won't anyone believe that?

Mate, I know Mum doesn't believe me. But, man, please believe me. It wasn't me. Or if it was, she pushed me to it. I dunno what she did, but she musta done somethin' pretty fucking extreme. You've gotta believe me. After, everythun I've told you she was capable of, you've gotta know I'm tellin' the truth… Maybe, manslaughter, but there's no way I should be in here for life…

Letter 16

S teve, the days have piled up now. I still think of 'er, but jail has a way of dullin' things, you know. It's been over fifteen years.

I've finished my high school certificate in here, Steve. I've learnt to read and write better. The pointlessness of it all is not so bad now. I barely wank anymore and the tattoos don't remind me of her like they used to. They're just there- marks on my arm, symbols of another life.

In the begginun, when the first letter came, I read it and re-read it, tryin' to find a clue- somethin' that would help get me outta here. It was pointless.

Every year (I never know which month it'll be), I get a letter from 'er stapled to the back of a 'With Compliments' slip from the legal firm that wrote 'er will. There's always a newspaper clippin' too. At first, it was kinda freaky mate- like she was talkun to me from beyond the grave, but I guess that's kinda the point. She always knew just how to press my buttons.

When they told me my son was coming to see me, I couldn't get up much enthusiasm. I am over fifty years old now. Some old-timers in 'ere reckon fifty's still young, but I gotta tell ya mate, I feel ancient. Is it like that for you? Is it old age that makes us think things are no longer as important as they used to seem? Or is that just a jail thing? I've been in here so long, I dunno about stuff like that anymore.

Michael came to see me today. I knew he was coming, but it's been so many years. The photo in my cell was taken when he was eight years old. He's twenty-somethin' now; nearly the same age as 'is mother when I met her. Fuck, he looks like her!

He didn't say a word at first, just slipped the letter across the table. It was dated before she died. Over fifteen years ago. There was some fancy letter from a lawyer saying this letter was going into trust.

And, here's the thing, Steve, I recognised the logo! That logo is on the 'With Compliments' slip that I've seen every year for the past fifteen years.

I looked up at Michael. He has his mother's eyes. I turned the page and –fuckin' hell! There it was! A newspaper clippin' from seven days before she died... so I knew this was another letter from 'er. I scanned the clippin':

Local News, 23 November 2009

A Coober Pedy man has been sentenced to seventeen years jail in Port Augusta. Leon Curtis used a wheel brace, a wheel rim, a pot and two stones to bash his partner to death. Curtis had a history of assaults against his partner.

I put the clippin' aside and then started readun her letter:-

Dear Michael,

*I*n the November after I left him, your father faced a court for the crime of assaulting me. He was fined $500.00 and placed on twelve months' probation for leaving behind bloody remnants of my skull to dry on a bare, white, brick kitchen wall. The way I see it, he was charged seventy cents a day for the two years of violence your brother and I endured.

When I found out I was dying, I agonised over whether it was time to tell you about my life with your father. This last month, as I have made the arrangements for meeting with your father (and for everything else that will happen afterwards), I have often found myself drawn to the sofa, where I used to be absorbed by those Michael Dransfield poems. Playing the DVD of your last soccer match from this past season over and over (do you remember how I captured you jumping up and high-fiving your team-mate, when you scored that winning goal?), I feel sad for all the things I will miss.

After countless re-runs of that clip, I have come to a decision. The boy scoring that goal is too young to know the truth, so this letter will be kept in trust with my solicitor. If things have gone according to plan, this letter has been with my solicitor for over fifteen years. You are a grown man, now. I hope you have had a good life (so far!) and have grown into the kind of man, who can make some peace with this.

Michael, your brother and I were terrorised by your father for two years of our lives. Knowing there was a chance you would end up experiencing the same unrelenting terror was the most devastating thing about being told I am dying.

Don't get me wrong, Michael. Everything about it pretty much sucks!

After all, I am thirty-four years old, as I write this, Michael, and I am never going to see you graduate primary school, let alone high school, or university. I am never going to get to see you get married or even win another soccer game with the under tens' team. (I hope you guys 'cream them', Michael, the season after I die and I hope you score the winning goal because we both know Russ can never resist buying you McDonald's when you do!).

Having some memories of you and Braydon growing up makes facing death feel okay, but not having more feels so unbelievably unjust! If I could trade those twenty-four months I spent with him (and still get to keep you as my son!) for just a few more memories, I think I'd do it in a heart-beat.

So, here's the thing, Michael, although this might make you angry at me, I am not writing this letter as an apologia or a justification. Only someone else who is told they are terminally ill can understand the enormity of it.

Although I work as a solicitor, I don't have a lot of faith in the system. From the moment they told me I was dying, I knew I would have to take care of this myself.

I don't know who raised you- if it was your Gran, or my Mum, or Russ like I wanted. But, Michael, as imperfect as life must have been for you, without a mother, being raised by any one of those people gave you a chance to turn out okay. With your father, there was no hope.

So, hopefully, the texts I have sent your father will help convict him. Tomorrow, he will come to my motel, unsure what to expect, maybe even a little frightened. If everything goes according to plan, I will seduce him and acquire the semen I need to pull the whole thing off.

Ensuring the methadone and heroin are untraceable has been surprisingly easy. As a lawyer, you get to know all sorts of people, Michael...

I plan to spike his beer with enough methadone to knock him out for the duration. Beer's good like that. You can barely taste the opiate bitterness. I intend to have my last shot of heroin, while it happens. For me, that seems a nice enough way to go.

There is no need to dishonour the dead. There are enough details in this account that what needs to be done can be done. Only the terminally ill can appreciate the enormity of leaving behind unfinished business.

I have left instructions for my body to be desecrated. I am supposed to be dead by the time it happens. So I don't expect to suffer.

The plan is for my syringe to be wiped, finger prints from your father's inert fingers to be pressed all over it. The same should happen with the knife. The contract about parental care is to be crumpled up using his hand.

I am taking away your chance to grow up, knowing your father. Michael, as callous as this may sound, I don't regret it.

But I am sorry that you will grow up with the stigma of having your mother murdered by your father, Michael. I am sorry for my part in that. And I know Russ well enough to know he has never forgiven me for arranging to see your father without consulting him. Please tell him this, for me, Michael: there was no way I could risk you growing up with your father.

I know that you will shoulder the biggest burden of my decision. I won't be there to wipe away the tears, when the kids are inevitably cruel. I am sorry Michael, but it is worth sacrificing twelve months of my life to make sure you will grow up safe.

I am dying on my own terms. During the two years I lived with your father, I never would have thought that was possible. Surely, that counts for something, right?

Forever, with love, your mother

Veronica Aranya

P.S. If you make the decision only you can make, tell him that, if he finally has the decency to tell the truth about our life together, that enough time has passed. Any additional prosecutions are unlikely. Let him know that's my legal opinion.

∗

Steve, I didn't want to cry in front of my son; not when it was the first time after so many years, I'd seen him. I couldn't help it. I burst out cryin'. I felt his hand on mine, but I couldn't look at him.

His voice had a hint of posh in it. He hadn't grown up local. He had gone to a good school, you could tell.

'It's okay, it's going to be all right.'

Epilogue

It was an odd collision of universes. But that was the story of her life, wasn't it?

Members of the judiciary mingled with solicitors; all of them exquisitely and appropriately dressed in expensive suits. Pete had been right in contending she was one of theirs.

A crew of 'alpha' women from the women's refuge, where she had once stayed, came to pay their respects. Armed with feminist attitude and purple tulips, dressed in various shades of cheese-cloth, they stood a little apart from police officers in starched blue uniforms.

There were many women and children in the crowd. Looking at them, Russ reflected that their presence would have pleased her.

Her father was there. A small, dark man in his sixties, dressed in a sharp, black suit, he looked grief-stricken. A decade punishing his daughter for being a junkie had taken its toll and Russ tried not to feel a small, mean-spirited sense of satisfaction about this.

Fiddling inanely with the keys in his pocket, Russ stared a little nervously at faces waiting expectantly for words he was sure would

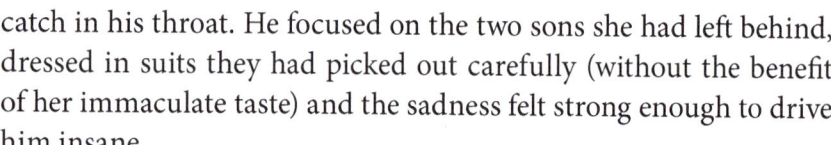

catch in his throat. He focused on the two sons she had left behind, dressed in suits they had picked out carefully (without the benefit of her immaculate taste) and the sadness felt strong enough to drive him insane.

She would have known every story. Every trauma became as much a part of her as her skin. Towards the end, Russ had wondered how he would penetrate the shell of sadness, but that didn't matter anymore.

Somewhere in the crowd, there was an eleven-year-old boy. When he had been six-years-old, the fury was too much for his tiny body to contain. He had yelled at Veronica, the first time he had met her, reaching for words to express the violence he had seen,

'You are a fucking cunt-whore-slut!'

A red-haired girl held her posy of daisies solemnly and was dressed in her Sunday, pastel yellow best. She stood beside her young, pretty, androgynously thin mother, who kept flicking the blonde fringe out of her eyes. Veronica could have told you that no one had taken Ella seriously, when she had said, casually, whilst chewing on sugar-free gum,

'Well, you know, he's kind of scary and, you know, he's kind of facing murder charges in another state.' Only Veronica saw the fear coated in the veneer of laid-back, Gen-Y flippancy.

Russ saw a sombrely dressed woman in the crowd, whose eyes looked almost as hard as his wife's had been. Veronica would have remembered her. She had been seven months' pregnant, when she came to Veronica's office. One of those ethereally radiant pregnant women, she was there to rehearse a statement. Veronica had not billed anyone for the time she had spent silently listening to this woman practicing the statement she would deliver the next day at the coronial inquest into the deaths of her children and the suicide of her ex-partner.

So, they buried these and other faint stories with ritualistic tosses of dirt over her coffin, when they buried Veronica Aranya. Searching for words to eulogise her, Russ felt the strange sensation of wanting to scrunch up this funeral scene, like a ball of paper, toss it away and start all over again. Looking into the sea of faces; some her fellow crusaders, some kindred survivors, he cleared his throat and began,

'V used to say it is always too much and never enough...'

www.ingramcontent.com/pod-product-compliance
Lightning Source LLC
Chambersburg PA
CBHW071358100726
47908CB00004B/1037